THE NURSE HE SHOULDN'T NOTICE

BY
SUSAN CARLISLE

First published in Great Britain 2012
by Mills & Boon, an imprint of Harlequin (UK) Limited.
Large Print edition 2013
Harlequin (UK) Limited, Eton House,
18-24 Paradise Road, Richmond, Surrey TW9 1SR

© Susan Carlisle 2012

ISBN: 978 0 263 23088 8

Harlequin (UK) policy is to use papers that are natural, renewable and recyclable products and made from wood grown in sustainable forests. The logging and manufacturing process conform to the legal environmental regulations of the country of origin.

Printed and bound in Great Britain
by CPI Antony Rowe, Chippenham, Wiltshire

He stepped into the kitchen, stopped cold, and shot to hot.

Maggie's back was to him and her hips were swaying to the beat of the music. Court's stomach contracted as if he'd been gut-punched. His pulse pounded in his ears. She wore shorts. Not an extremely tall woman, she still had the longest, shapeliest, sexiest legs he'd ever seen.

He gulped. Oh, yes, he was a leg man, all right—and Maggie had an outstanding pair. What would it be like to have one of those wrapped around him in bed?

Mercy, he was losing it. Had he been out in the heat too long?

Had her keeping her legs hidden so well under skirts made them even more appealing? Was it because they were forbidden, or because they were Maggie's? He wanted to believe the former true, but he wouldn't bet on it. He knew lust when he felt it. He was a red-blooded male and he appreciated women.

But Maggie was the type of woman who led with her heart. He'd seen it more than once as she cared for patients during clinic. His feelings were securely vaulted away. He didn't do relationships…

Dear Reader

Often when we stop focusing on ourselves and start concentrating on others good things happen that we never dreamed were possible. Too many times we become so secure in our own world that we must step out beyond our comfort zone to change our perspective. When we do that we are more aware of others around us, and that can make a difference in our own lives. My characters, Court and Maggie, are no different from us. They must struggle, but they find the truth in the saying 'Give and it will be returned to you.'

Although the hospital in Teligu is fictitious, and Maggie and Court's story comes completely out of my imagination, there *are* dedicated and hard-working doctors and nurses who spend their lives working to provide healthcare to the people in the remote areas of northern Ghana. You can find out more about the medical work being done there on my website: www.SusanCarlisle.com

I hope you enjoy Court and Maggie's love story as much as I enjoyed telling it.

Susan Carlisle

Susan Carlisle's love affair with books began when she made a bad grade in maths in the sixth grade. Not allowed to watch TV until she brought the grade up, she filled her time with books and became a voracious romance reader. She has 'keepers' on her shelf to prove it. Because she loved the genre so much, she decided to try her hand at creating her own romantic worlds. She still loves a good happily-ever-after story.

When not writing Susan doubles as a high school substitute teacher, which she has been doing for sixteen years. Susan lives in Georgia with her husband of twenty-eight years, and has four grown children. She loves castles, travelling, cross-stitching, hats, James Bond and hearing from her readers.

Why not check out Susan's fantastic debut for Mills & Boon® Medical Romance™?

HEART SURGEON, HERO…HUSBAND?

Also available in eBook format from www.millsandboon.co.uk

My special thanks go to:
My Tuesday night critique group for all your advice.
Dr. Chupp for giving medical details.
Sia Huff and Carol Burnside
for being such great critique partners.
Flo Nicoll for being such a supportive editor.

CHAPTER ONE

THE dry season dust surged past Maggie Everett as she halted the battered Jeep next to the sleek jet. Raising a hand, she shielded her eyes from the sun and the haze of the plains of northern Ghana in West Africa.

As the passengers disembarked from the plane, one in particular drew her attention. Maggie hadn't seen many American men near her age of twenty-eight in the last couple of years but she could still recognize a fine-looking specimen when she saw one.

He looked in her direction, while behind him the three other newcomers sorted out their luggage. A balding man pointed and issued orders while pulling boxes and baggage from the belly of the aircraft. Two young women, chatting with excitement, searched through bundles that were unloaded. They must be the nursing students who'd be working during their summer break from college.

These were the latest medical personnel to fill in at the remote hospital for a few weeks. She appreciated the assistance but what the hospital desperately needed was enough financial support to hire additional physicians who would be committed to staying for years.

The man caught her full attention again as he strode toward her. His aviator sunglasses added mystique. Slim-hipped, wide-shouldered and, if she had to guess, over six feet. He reminded her of the guys in those year-old magazines her mother sent in care packages. Like one of the models from a cologne ad. An undertone of ruggedness, offset by a touch of refinement. Maggie's pulse beat a little faster in anticipation.

Reaching her, he flipped the glasses up to rest on the top of his head, revealing crystal-blue eyes, made sharper by the deep tan of his skin. "I'm Dr. Court Armstrong. I've two sensitive pieces of equipment that need to be seen about right away."

No hello, nice to meet you. His crisp New England accent caught her off guard. Could he be? "Armstrong? As in the Armstrong Foundation?

Boston?" She didn't try to keep her disgust out of her voice.

"Yes."

He could be the very one who had denied the hospital's request for aid, including her plan for an urgently needed children's clinic. The locals were desperate for medical care, children the most. The hospital required help to stay open, and her new program could make a difference. But the hospital didn't meet their requirements for funds. It was in too remote an area, not seeing enough patients. She gritted her teeth. Not qualify! She couldn't imagine a project more qualified or a hospital more in need.

"So why are you here if you've already denied our application?"

His mouth compressed for a second before he said, "I'll be glad to discuss that with you after we get this equipment out of the sun."

Before she could respond with the sharp retort that sprang to mind, her name filled the air.

"Missy Maggie, Missy Maggie." Neetie, a young African boy, ran across the parched ground toward her. Clouds of dust trailed behind. He halted beside the Jeep. "Truck. Hit. Hurt," he said in his native tongue between panting breaths. "Come. Now."

"You're needed," she said to the doctor. "Get in, Neetie."

The long-legged doctor gave a curt nod and picked up a knapsack from the pile of luggage before climbing into the seat beside her. Maggie noted his split-second hesitation before he reached for Neetie.

Using one arm, Dr. Armstrong swung the boy into the back and called over his shoulder, "John, see to the machines." Turning to her, he said, "Let's go." He returned his dark glasses to their place on his nose. She missed the clear blue coolness of his eyes. What a shame to hide those pools, and an even greater shame they belonged to such an insufferable man.

The Jeep cranked on the first turn of the key. Maggie floored the gas and the vehicle shot forward. She steered a circle around the plane and back toward the compound. "Where, Neetie?" The wind whipped the words away.

"In front of Arthur's."

Dr. Armstrong gripped the edge of the windshield, one foot propped on the raised edge, a hand on his bag as if he wasn't comfortable racing to an emergency in an emerging country. After he realized the conditions he'd have to practice medicine in, she wouldn't be surprised if twenty-four hours from now, he took off in that fancy jet, looking for his pressed-white-lab-coat world again.

She slid the Jeep to a stop in front of the hospital. When Dr. Armstrong's hand slapped against the dash to stop his forward motion, Maggie's mouth lifted slightly at the corners.

"Why're we—?"

"Supplies." She gathered up a handful of her skirt's material, climbing out of the Jeep. This was one of those times when the clothes she was required to wear were a nuisance.

Minutes later, Maggie returned with a large black bag she kept prepared for this type of situation.

Dr. Armstrong jumped out and met her. "I'll take that," he said, reaching for the bag. He placed it beside Neetie.

Before she put the Jeep in gear he'd returned to his seat.

Maggie said nothing to her passengers as she drove. Instead she concentrated on weaving her way through streets lined with clay-brick, one-story buildings and filled with people and animals. She glanced at the man beside her. The doctor made no attempt to speak either, seeming to absorb everything around him.

Reaching the accident, she could see that a truck had hit a cart. People mingled around an elderly man who must have been pushing the cart. He lay off to the side, clutching his chest, while a child of about nine had her legs pinned beneath the cart. A woman chattered in a loud voice at the man standing beside the truck.

Maggie's stomach clenched. She hated to see a child hurt most of all. No matter how far she ran, she still couldn't outrun her mothering nature when a child was in trouble.

The Jeep had almost come to a jolting stop when Dr. Armstrong's feet touched the ground. Slinging his pack over his shoulder, he lifted the other bag from the back. "You check the child. I'll take the old man. Looks like a heart attack."

Well, he certainly had no trouble giving orders! Who did he think he was to drop out of the sky and five minutes later start telling her what to do? As lead nurse, she'd been the one who'd made most of the daily decisions. She knew what to do, and didn't need super-Doc to take over before he'd even seen the hospital in Teligu. She made no comment regarding his high-handedness. Having someone in charge during an emergency was critical to maintaining order, and Dr. Armstrong made it clear he believed that was him. "Neetie, you go with Mr. Doctor. Talk for him," she instructed the boy.

Going to the girl, Maggie used a gentle voice hoping to calm her fears. Her ex-emergency-room nurse instincts took over. Quickly she assessed the girl's injuries while keeping an eye on the doctor's progress. She couldn't have a newbie fresh off the plane damage the relationship and trust that the hospital had painstakingly built with these people.

He gave curt, simple directions that Neetie translated from a distance, as if the doctor had placed Neetie in that spot, not too far away but not too close.

Using hand gestures, Maggie instructed three men on how to raise the cart off the child. Maggie pulled the girl out by the shoulders and then examined the girl's injured right leg.

Dr. Armstrong joined her. "Thankfully no heart

issues. The man's forehead will require stitches but those can wait. I applied a couple of four-by-four gauze bandages and told Neetie to tell him to hold them in place. The girl?"

"Fractured leg," Maggie said, not looking at him. "Thank God that appears to be the only injury."

He pulled the supply bag over to him and knelt across the girl from Maggie. The doctor ran long tapered fingers over the girl's distended skin with medical thoroughness but something was missing. No soothing voice, no tender touch, no personal involvement. His actions were all strictly clinical. "Let's get this stabilized and get her to the hospital."

Despite the negative emotions his last name and attitude kindled in her, Maggie grudgingly admitted he seemed to know his medical care despite his almost non-existent bedside manner. Still, he wasn't going to push her out of the way as if this was her first day in Ghana, instead of his.

Maggie handed him splints. He gave her a quick glance of admiration. She squeezed the girl's hand, before holding one of the boards in place while the doctor gripped the other.

Pursing her lips, she drew in a breath. The pain in the girl's eyes pulled at Maggie's heart. She reassured the girl that she would be fine. If it hadn't been for her own accident, Maggie might have been the mother of a little girl close to the same age. Because she couldn't have her own children, she'd embraced each native child as hers. She even planned to adopt Neetie. It made her livid to think about how much she could do for them if the Armstrong Foundation would support the hospital. "The bandage is in the right-hand corner of the bag, Dr. Armstrong."

He reached for it. Passing the material back and forth, they slowly began to wrap it around the boards holding the leg straight.

"You make my surname sound like a dirty word. Why don't you call me Court?"

"What?" she asked, distracted by her thoughts of getting the bandage just right.

"My name. After an emergency—what, less than five minutes after I land?—I think we can survive on a first-name basis. And you're Missy Maggie."

Her usually efficient movements faltered when his fingers slid over hers as he handed her the wrapping. "I'm Maggie Everett. *The* head nurse. You can call me Maggie."

He glanced at her as she returned the wrapping. With deft movements suggesting years of practice, he secured the end by tucking it under the edge of the material. Without looking at the girl, he said, "Maggie, tell her that we are taking her to the hospital."

No "please" there but Maggie did as he instructed, then went to move the Jeep closer. She couldn't fault the new doctor's care, but she was used to the visiting doctors showing more personal attention, more personal interaction with patients. He was no different than his family's foundation.

The people of Teligu needed help and this man had the influence to see they got it. Could she convince him to persuade the foundation to reverse its decision?

Court stepped into the cool evening. He ran his hands through his hair and took a deep breath. The air smelled fresh compared to the busy city of Boston. Even the noises of the night were a sharp contrast to those of home. He took a moment to listen to the wildlife bickering back and forth, and the shuffles of an animal searching for food outside the compound fence. He'd never call this place home.

Was Ghana something like his parents had experienced all those years ago? Part of what had kept them going on medical mission trips even when his mother had become pregnant? He shook his head. His parents should have been in the States, not off in the wild, especially with his mother so far along.

He shook his head. With his kind of luck, his first patient in Ghana had to be a young girl. He'd not trusted himself with a child's care since that awful night. The girl had required his attention and he'd had no choice but to tend her. The constant reminder to focus ticker-taping through his mind kept his hands steady.

The soft casting of the girl's leg hadn't been challenging. Yet he felt exhausted. He'd flown all day, crossed three time zones and was coming down from the adrenaline rush of an emergency. It did feel good to be practicing medicine again, even if he had to start with a child. Still, he needed sleep.

Heck, he didn't even know where he was to bunk. Scanning the compound, he didn't see anyone to ask. The screen door behind him slammed, and Maggie stepped out.

They'd worked well together, despite his feeling that she didn't like him. He'd been impressed by her efficiency in casting the girl's leg regardless of the rudimentary exam room and equipment. She did everything with precision and care. In America, these facilities would be comparable to a back-alley clinic. Like the one he and his brother had been born in. The one without enough technology to help his brother. Now wasn't the time to start dredging up those ugly, negative memories. He pushed them back into the corner of his mind where they belonged.

Even with the events of the past few hours, Maggie still had a fresh look about her. Her dark, wavy hair was pulled high on her head and brushed the top of her shoulders. What would it be like down? A dark flowing waterfall? In the dim light, he could just make out her quizzical expression. Had he voiced his curiosity out loud?

"I guess you'd like to settle in." Her business-like voice eclipsed the evening sounds. "I'll show you to your bungalow. Someone will have already put your bags there." She didn't sound as if she welcomed the chore.

"I could use some rest. Long day and even longer evening."

"I'd like to tell you a day like today is unusual but it isn't." She stepped away and headed down a winding path.

Her look implied she'd expected a negative reaction. "Have I done something to make you angry?"

"*Your* foundation has done something to these people." She stopped. Her words were cutting as she spread her arm out in a dramatic arc. "The hospital requested support and we were denied!"

"Now, Ms. Everett, you know the foundation must make tough decisions. We would like to give—"

"Don't patronize me and don't give me the party line. From what you've seen today, can you think of another medical facility that needs help more?" Her voice rose with her ire.

He found Maggie even more interesting fired up and fighting. "To be honest, I need to spend more time here to answer that question." He brushed his hand across his forehead slick with sweat, even in the night air. All he wanted right now was a bath and bed.

"Cop-out," she huffed. The words hung between them for a second before she asked, "By the way, are you on the foundation board?"

He took a deep breath. She wasn't going to like his answer. "Yes, I'm the acting CEO."

Her shoulders squared and her back went straight as a pole. "So you knew the foundation had turned the hospital down before you came here." She almost spat the words.

"I did. I also read your appeal letter. It's why I'm here." Her impassioned plea for the foundation to reconsider its decision had touched a chord in him. He'd decided to come and see for himself if all she'd written was true, if perhaps he could finally do some good. Still, he had no intention of telling her the other reasons he'd come to this desolate place. Like making a decision about whether or not to continue practicing medicine. "I thought I'd see what the hospital's needs were for myself. The foundation receives numerous applications for assistance but we can't fulfill them all. Not every request has merit."

"I can assure you ours does."

"I've yet to make that determination."

She looked him square in the eyes. "Then I'll have to convince you." She glanced away, then said, "You don't practice medicine?"

"I'm a trained pediatrician but I've taken a leave of absence. The foundation takes all my time right now."

He'd stopped practicing when he'd allowed a little boy and his parents to suffer for his inattentiveness. The boy now lived with brain damage, just as Court's brother had. Court should've gone when he'd been paged but he had been too busy with foundation business, trying to make points with his parents. Trying to fill some juvenile need to be noticed. Even thinking about it disgusted him. A grown man should've gotten over it by now. But he'd hurt a child. Everyone said that Jimmy's reaction to the meds wasn't his fault but they would never convince him. Either way, there was still a child living as his brother had because of *him*.

"Really?"

"Why the sound of surprise?"

"You were good enough with the girl today, but you don't act like the typical ped doc."

Ouch, Missy Maggie was way too perceptive. He'd thought he'd covered up how anxious he'd been while seeing to the child. "How's that?"

"I don't know how to explain it. I've seen all kinds of doctors come through here and I can usually tell by how they interact with a patient what field they're in. I've not missed one in a long time."

"Well, it's nice to know that there's still some mystery to me."

Maggie shrugged before she started down the worn dirt path toward a copse of squat, low-canopied trees. "The bungalows are out this way."

He watched the soft sway of her hips under her long cotton skirt. All the women here wore some type of flowing skirt or dress. Hers was too lengthy to give him any more than a glimpse of well-formed calf. She wasn't waiting to see if he followed.

"Have you worked here long?" he asked as he caught up with her.

"I've been working in the Teligu Hospital for

a little more than two years." The words flowed over her delicate shoulder.

"And you're already the head nurse?"

She chuckled low in her throat. "Yeah, and sometimes nutritionist, health inspector and ward housekeeper. Around here we do it all."

Her dry mirth punctuated her earlier anger. "We all pitch in. Locals are hired to do some of the work but there's always something needing to be done. Like today."

"How many are on staff?"

She turned round, her eyes having gone serious. "Including you and me? Not enough."

"Why not?"

"For the same reason you're only here for a short while." She looked out across the compound as if taking it in for the first time. "Lack of super-markets, malls and night life…" Her voice trailed off into a soft, accepting voice, which told Court she'd run out of energy to fight.

He said nothing for a while. For some reason he wished he could commit to staying forever just to see her happy. That was an odd thought. "So what does the hospital need most?"

"Doctors. Not for a couple of weeks or months.

Staff willing to commit to staying for a year or more. Pharmacists, nurses, a hospital director, or any other medical professional you can think of, we could use them all. And the money to encourage them to stay longer and..." she paused for effect "...a children's clinic."

"What about doctors and nurses local to the area?" He would continue to pepper her with questions as long as she agreed to answer them.

"No native doctors. For pretty much the same reason others don't stay." Her voice strengthened, a steel edge entering it with her passion for the subject. "If they get out of the villages, they find they like the life at the coast. And the money. There're five full-time nurses. We're training local women, and some go off to school with the help of the government."

"Doctors?"

"Just Dr. Roberts full time, we fill in with visiting doctors. For the next couple of weeks it will be Dr. Roberts and you. But Dr. Roberts will take a few days of vacation next week. He's not had any time off in months." She finished with a flourish.

The more she spoke, the more animated Maggie became. He couldn't take his eyes off the petite woman who spoke like a lioness protecting her young. What would it be like to have someone who loved so unconditionally in his corner?

Court leaned back. "We've more help. Another doctor flew in with me."

"Really?" She seemed excited by the news. "Great. We'll be able to do the clinic in one of the neighboring villages after all."

They'd reached a simple, cinder-block structure, covered by a tin roof. She opened the screen door and held it for him. He stepped into the tile-floored room. A lamp illuminated two well-used chairs and a small bare table in the sitting area. A ceiling fan produced the only air circulation.

"There's a small kitchen area, bedroom and bath through there." She pointed in the direction of a dark doorway.

Her skirt brushed against his cargo pants as he moved to tug on a light pull so he could see down the hall.

She shifted, putting distance between them. "You can fix your own meals or we've a mess hall. Since there's no food stored here, I'll be by at six-thirty in the morning to show you where you get breakfast. If we have a few minutes before rounds, I'll take you around the hospital. Clinic starts promptly at seven-thirty."

Her words were all but rolling over each other. Did he make her nervous? He would've never imagined anyone could rattle this unflappable woman.

Stepping out the door, she warned, "Be sure and latch the screen before you go to bed."

Maggie was running. And she wasn't half as impressed with him as he'd like. She certainly shared no love for his family's philanthropic endeavors. Missy Maggie reminded him of his favorite kind of candy, hard on the outside, gooey in the center. He'd like to find out what other surprises she hid.

The next morning Court started down the bungalow's short hall as a knock sounded at the door.

Maggie stood outside the screened entry. She wore a scooped-neck shirt and a floral skirt, hiding what he imagined were enticing curves. Her chestnut hair hung from the nape of her neck secured by a rubber band. She looked shiny, natural and young. And completely out of place in this stark land.

"I didn't think you'd be up," she said through the wire mesh.

"You told me six-thirty, and it's six-thirty." He pushed the door open, stepping out.

The glint in her eye suggested she might be laughing at him. "We'll see if you feel this chipper tomorrow morning."

He still felt the same chill from her that had been present the day before. He fell into step beside her as they took a different path from last night. This one ended at a long, low building adjacent to the hospital.

"This is what we affectionately call the mess hall." She led the way to a short buffet line set up at one end.

It resembled a military mess hall he'd seen in pictures.

"The food's prepared for the in-patients Monday through Saturday. Families bring the meals in on Sunday. Most of us find it easier to eat here than to go to the town market daily." After filling her plate, she moved toward an empty table.

"Hey, Court," John Weber, the doctor who had flowm in with him, called. "Come join us. Tell us where you disappeared to yesterday."

"Sure." He and Maggie took chairs at the table. "Maggie, you haven't had a chance to meet John Weber. He works with the foundation. This is Lisa Mills and Jen Skindowski." He directed a hand toward first the blonde and then the brunette woman sitting beside the doctor.

She nodded to the women and shook hands with John. "I'm sorry. I thought you were the pilot."

John laughed. "No, I'm a general practitioner. The pilot would be Court. It's his jet."

Court shrugged when her piercing gaze came back to him. She didn't look impressed. Did she think he should sell the plane and offer the money to the hospital?

"In fact, you could call it his baby, he loves it so much." John took a bite of scrambled egg.

"I imagine a plane makes it easy to get around," she mumbled. What she left unsaid made him uncomfortable.

"John, did you get the equipment taken care of?"

"Yeah, the director put it in storage. I made sure it was handled carefully. So tell me about the big emergency yesterday." John kept his focus on Court.

"Truck and cart accident. Cart lost. A child with a clean fracture. An old man who needed a couple of stitches. The girl was doing well when I checked on her at midnight."

Maggie's head jerked up. "You went to check on her in the middle of the night?"

"Don't sound so shocked. I like to keep a personal eye on my patients." He'd failed to check on a patient once and he'd never make that mistake again, even if he was still a long way from feeling comfortable around children. She gave a nod of approval. It felt good to think her opinion of him had taken at least a slight upturn. Something about how she'd reacted to the girl being injured made him believe the children routinely received her special attention.

Lisa asked Maggie a question about the facility, and they began discussing the hospital and the area. There were additional questions about the people and the type of care they most often required. Court listened, impressed by how involved Maggie was with her patients. She clearly loved her work and the Mamprusi people.

She pushed her plate away and said to the group, "If you're finished, why not join Court for a tour?"

Court lagged behind the others as Maggie pointed out buildings within the compound.

She turned to the nurses. "Don't go outside the fence after dark and only with a companion during the day. It isn't like at home. There's no police or law like you're used to."

Inside the hospital building she pointed out the pharmacy, office area, supply area, and the two ORs. She led them to the women's ward where the beds looked to be World War II surplus. Family members were sitting or sleeping on the floor around their loved ones.

Jen asked, "Why're there people everywhere?"

"We ask families to help care for their loved ones. There's not enough staff to do it all," Maggie explained.

Had he been wrong in his evaluation of the hospital's application? Maybe, but he wasn't ready to concede that so early in the visit. He couldn't let her emotional play on the situation get in the way of a comprehensive evaluation.

The men's and the children's wards were much the same. Leaving the latter, Maggie stopped and looked straight at Court. "You're the pediatrician so you need to know we don't tell the parents if their child is dying because they'll desert them."

If her intent was to drive home the point the hospital could use foundation money to hire additional stuff, she'd done it. With one-two punches.

He'd been born in a small jungle clinic but he'd been reared around glistening state-of-the-art hospitals in Boston. Aware of the type of work the foundation supported, he'd still never been in a hospital this primitive.

"It's time for rounds," Maggie said. "Lisa and Jen, I'll leave you to help out in the children's ward. One of the staff members will show you what needs to be done. Doctors, we'll meet Dr. Roberts in the men's ward."

Court looked out the window of the hallway linking the two buildings while they walked. The line of people waiting, sitting or standing stretched as far as he could see. He couldn't keep the amazement out of his voice. "Are all those people waiting to be seen?"

"Yes. We see around three hundred a day. And do eight to twelve surgeries."

He whistled. She made it sound like there was nothing to it.

She met his look. "Another reason we have difficulty keeping doctors and nurses."

They entered the men's ward. "Dr. Roberts, I brought you help. Gentlemen, I'll see you later in clinic." Maggie turned and left.

Maggie looked across the packed dirt yard in the direction of the patient clinic. She scanned the crowd of people waiting in the open-air treatment area. With relief, she spotted Court's dark-haired head. He had stepped out of the building, deep in conversation with one of the local orderlies who spoke English.

She hadn't spoken to Court since earlier in the morning. Lunch was taken in shifts, so she had no idea how his day was going. She'd bet he wouldn't have any trouble sleeping tonight. A couple of times from a distance she'd had a chance to watch him work. His personality didn't endear him to her but she'd grudgingly admit he was a good doctor, maybe one of the best they'd seen in some time.

He stopped speaking to the tall man, looked up and met her gaze, like he'd known she needed him. A tingle zipped along her spine. She waved him in her direction and walked to meet him halfway.

There were two small furrows between his brows. "Is something wrong?"

Her voice lowered. "I need you to look at a wound. I've been checking it weekly but it doesn't seem to be improving." She led him toward a young woman sitting on a portable examination table.

"Raja, this is Dr. Armstrong," Maggie said. "He's going to look at your leg." Court gave Raja a reassuring smile. "Tell her I would like her to lie back," he said to Maggie.

She relayed his message.

Court supported Raja's back as he helped her lie back on the table. Maggie moved to the other side of the table, facing him.

He raised the cloth bandage from the wound. The smell of infection wafted into the air. Maggie saw the slight jerk of Court's cheek only because she watched him. She was grateful he didn't let on to the frightened Raja how bad the situation was.

Apparently his bedside manner extended to women if not children. If he didn't like children then why in the world had he become a pediatrician? That ironic twist made him interesting for some reason. Was there more going on with Dr. Armstrong than he was letting on?

Court touched the skin around the worst area of the injury.

"How did this happen?" His eyes flickered upward toward her for a second, before his attention returned to Raja's leg.

"The water barrel she'd been carrying on her head slipped. As it fell it hit her leg, making a gash. She lives so far away she didn't come in to get it stitched."

He looked up. Their gazes met. Held. The confirmation of her diagnosis showed in his eyes. His stone-faced look was the opposite of the emotional upheaval she felt. A mixture of sorrow, pain and disappointment all rolled within her.

Didn't he have any feelings about what was going to happen to Raja? Maggie blinked. At least he could show some regret for what was to come.

Court spoke to Raja again and helped her to sit up. "Maggie, could I speak to you a moment?"

They stepped a few paces away before Court stopped. "You do know the leg has to come off, don't you?"

Maggie nodded, looking at the ground.

"It's too far gone. If she didn't live in these deplorable conditions…" A tone of remorse filled his voice. "Why didn't you say something to Dr. Roberts about this earlier?"

Maggie's head jerked up and she met his gaze. "Don't be too quick to issue blame. Around here the people have to work hard every day to eke out some kind of existence." The hopelessness of the situation, her inability to make a real difference washed over her but she bowed her back and continued. "Coming to us means giving up a day of labor, and sometimes walking ten miles or more. When they get here they have to wait in line for hours because we're so short-staffed. It's not that they don't want help, it's just that it takes so much effort to get it. And as for me not informing Dr. Roberts, I did. He and I have been doing all we can."

"I didn't understand—"

"No, you didn't. You need to be here longer than twenty-four hours before you start judging us." All of a sudden she felt tired to the bone. Her shoulders slumped. Just one night she'd like to fall asleep knowing she'd offered the best medical care possible in the world. That would never happen here.

Court stared at her a moment. "I wish I knew another way but if her leg isn't removed then the gangrene could spread and kill her. Do you want me to tell her?"

With your emotionally distant attitude, I don't think so. "She's my friend. I'll explain." Maggie turned to go back to Raja but jumped when Court's hand on her shoulder stopped her. His touch comforted. For a second his eyes showed a glimpse of compassion before they became shuttered again.

"I wish it didn't have to be this way."

He sounded as if he meant it. Maybe the ice doctor did have a heart. "I do too," she said. His hand fell away when she turned back to Raja.

CHAPTER TWO

COURT ran a hand across his face. Swiveling his head from side to side, he worked the kinks out of his neck. He gazed into the night sky. It'd been a long, horrible day. He'd done a rotation in the largest emergency room in Boston but nothing had compared to the volume of people this primitive clinic saw each day. This hospital needed at least two more full-time physicians.

He'd expected to have to care for patients on this trip but nothing like the magnitude he'd been presented with that day. And the number of children. It was almost overwhelming. With great fortitude he'd managed to care for the first one through to the twentieth. Thankfully his training went into autopilot mode and he found some semblance of comfort, a return of a modicum of confidence. Still, he'd be lying if he said he wasn't glad to see the day done.

Finished with the last patient, he'd headed to the

mess hall for a bite to eat. Dr. Roberts had come by and asked him to assist with removing Raja's leg. Court had explained he wasn't qualified. Dr. Roberts responded, "Here we do it all. I'll show you where to scrub in."

The surgery had been short and unpleasant. He always thought an operation helped. It fixed. In this case, a life had been saved yet devastated. The only saving grace was that Maggie hadn't been there with those big accusing eyes. She had to be thinking—if *he* hadn't turned the hospital down for funds, if *he* could see the need for outlying clinics, if *he* could get the supplies they needed…

Had he been a part of making a wrong decision that had hurt someone? Guilt gnawed at him, becoming a living entity in his gut that grew stronger by feeding on his doubts. He wanted to feel good about himself again, wanted to see respect for him shinning in someone's eyes—Maggie's.

But why should he care what she thought? He wasn't going to get involved with her. That would be opening a door to hurt that he didn't need, refused to accept. He'd learned at an early age that when you cared for someone you got hurt. If you didn't want to hurt, you kept your heart and feelings locked away. Missy Maggie wouldn't be allowed to knock on that door. Getting involved with Miss Save the World was out of the question. He had larger things to worry about in his life than trying to please her. Like what direction his career would take when he returned to Boston.

Court trudged along the path toward his bungalow by moonlight, too wired to sleep. Something moved among the trees. Stopping, he squinted in an effort to determine if it was man or beast. He'd heard talk of animals finding their way under and over the chain-link fence at night. Maggie had even made a point of warning him to lock his door.

Stepping closer, he found Maggie, sitting in a hammock. He left the path, walking with caution over the uneven ground with its dry grass clumps. The night shade flung shadows across the earth.

Maggie glanced at him as he approached. "Hey," she said in a low voice, but not one of real welcome.

"What're you doing out here so late?" He eased closer, trying to get a better look at her face. "You okay?"

She didn't say anything for a long moment. "Yeah."

Her flip-flop dropped from her foot. He wouldn't have noticed the action except for the sparkle of rhinestones. Yet another contradiction to his first impression of her. Miss All Business, Give Me the Facts had a quirky side. Interesting.

Stabbing her big toe into the half dirt, half dried-up grass, she pushed backward in the hammock.

"Raja's resting well," Court said into the quiet night.

"Good."

Her almost non-existent answer screamed of her distress.

"You know..." she pushed the hammock back and swung forward again "...women in this land are the family workhorses, carrying water for long distances, gathering food and building homes."

Court spied a wooden chair beside a tree. He sat, arms resting on his knees, content to listen while she talked. Her voice had a pleasant, lyrical quality that soothed.

Maggie sighed. "A woman without a leg is dependent on the village to keep her alive. Her husband will put her out. She's no use to him."

She sobbed softly, her empathy for the woman almost a personal pain. Something in the sound of her sorrow suggested the grief went deep. Had someone done something similar to her?

The desire to wrap Maggie in his arms surprised him. The emotion was so foreign that he hardly recognized it for what it was. The tug was so strong he gripped the edge of the chair.

"I came here to help." Her words were a murmur crossing the hot still air. "To make a difference. But I don't see it happening. I told Raja what to do. Showed her how to bandage it…"

She raised her eyes to the starry heavens. "I appreciate you taking care of her."

"You're welcome." He'd not felt so inadequate since that horrible night he'd failed his small patient. His jaw tightened. Caring wasn't a feeling he would make a habit. He'd been running from his emotions since his brother had died and now he'd come smack up against them again. Heaven help him, for some reason this woman managed to pull them out of him.

She pushed into a slow swing. "So what did you think about clinic today?"

He sat up in the chair. "I'm more than impressed

by the number of people seen and the vast array of medical issues needing treatment."

Maggie dug her toe into the ground, bringing the hammock to a halt. She gave him a look he was confident would make a weaker person squirm and give up information.

"So, now you think we could use the grant?"

He put up his hand. "Ho, there. I didn't say that. There're many hospitals and programs needing money, a number closer to home. What I will say is I've been impressed with how efficiently the hospital runs with so few obvious resources."

"Well, at least that's something. Hopefully we'll continue to impress you with our service, and you'll see our need." She scooted to the edge of the hammock.

The movement captured his attention, her hips shifting first one way then the other as she wiggled to the edge, supporting herself by holding on to the side. Not for the first time he longed to see her legs. What was the old saying? "Leave them wanting more?" Maggie had definitely perfected that objective.

She slipped her feet into the flip-flops. "It's

late." She made an attempt to stand but fell into the hammock as it swung backward.

Court offered his hand. "Let me help you." Her low-trilled laugh of embarrassment vibrated through him like a bow moving across the string of a bass violin.

Her hand hovered over his palm. For a second he feared she'd refuse his help. When her fingers touched his, the bolt of satisfaction stunned him.

Using him for leverage, Maggie pulled herself to her feet. She stood so close he could make out the faint wildflower smell of her shampoo. It was the most surprising thing he'd encountered in this arid land. It stood out in the surroundings like Maggie did.

What was her story? She seemed full of contradictions.

Maggie slid her hand from his, leaving him with a sense of loss. Gathering up her skirt in a hand so it no longer flowed around her legs, she headed toward their bungalows.

"I've been meaning to ask why the female staff wears long skirts in this heat." He stepped over a protruding root.

She grinned over her shoulder.

The first real one he'd seen since he'd arrived.

"Wearing a skirt is cooler and more functional than you'll ever believe. You should try one. Local men wear them all the time."

He chuckled. "No, thanks, I'll stick with scrubs and cargo pants."

"The real reason we wear them…" she did an about-face and looked him straight in the eye "…is because the Mamprusi men find female thighs sexy. In America, breasts seem to be the thing, here it's thighs."

Court agreed with the Mamprusi.

She'd delivered the teasing bit of information like she gave a report during medical rounds. The upward curve to her lips and the slight shake of her shoulders said she wanted to laugh. "Do you have any other questions, Doctor?"

"No-o-o, I think that about sums it up."

She giggled. A sense of rightness filled him—something he'd not felt in a long time.

They reached the spot in the path where they'd separate to go to their respective bungalows.

He touched her arm briefly to get her attention. "Hey, would you give me a crash course in Manprusi? It would sure make treating the patients easier if I learned a few basic words. Help put them at ease."

"I guess so." She turned, starting down the path.

In a couple of strides he caught up with her. "How about tomorrow afternoon? I understand the clinic's closed," he said. "I was wondering if you'd show me around the village, maybe give me a lesson then. I'd like to know more about the people. I don't think the wild ride yesterday counted as a true visit."

She took longer than he would have liked to answer. "I guess so. I planned to get some fruit and other items at the market anyway."

"Aw, thanks for having compassion for the new guy in town."

That brought a slight curve to her lips. Court watched as she walked to her door a few steps away, rubbing the spot he'd touched.

Maggie had been a little surprised when Court hadn't balked at walking into the village when she'd suggested it. He acted like he made casual outings to a village regularly. While they moved along the crowded dusty road, she appreciated him matching his long-legged pace to her shorter one.

He hadn't struck her as someone who routinely

took time for a stroll but she couldn't miss a chance to have him see up close how the locals lived and why they needed the Armstrong Foundation's help. Convincing him to use his influence to give the hospital the funds they required was her primary objective. Otherwise she would've turned him down flat when he'd asked her to show him around. Something about having him close made her think she wouldn't be enjoying a few relaxing hours. Court set her nerves tingling.

Court impressed her with his thoughtful and intelligent questions about the traditions and culture. Between his quizzing and her lectures on the area, they practiced simple words like "hello", "pain", "where", "how long" in Mamprusi. He was a quick study, which by this time didn't surprise her. He had a real aptitude for the difficult language. It wasn't long before she expanded to using phases.

Maggie glanced inside the doorways of the simple square, dirt-brick buildings facing each other creating a wide main road. She pointed to one group. "These are the well-to-do businesses. Most of the locals live humbly, working daily just to stay alive."

He seemed genuinely interested in the country's history and the people. The closer they drew to the market, the more the number of people surrounding them increased. The sounds of bargaining filled the air, joining the ripe smell of fruit. "Stay close, I don't want to lose you," she said, turning a corner into a large open area filled with stalls. Colorful fruit, vegetables and a variety of meats were spread out in the open air on blankets with thin men squatting on their haunches beside their goods.

"You don't think a tall, white man dressed in American clothing is going to stand out?"

With his piercing blue eyes, firm jaw and broad shoulders he'd stand out on the streets of New York City. The man was eye candy. "You have a point. Is there anything you'd like to look for while we're here?"

"No, but I would like to practice what I've learnt when I can. I'll just stick by your side."

She wasn't sure why the statement rattled her so much. "I'm not sure *Where does it hurt?* or *Bandage it this way* is going to work here."

"I was thinking, *Hello, goodbye, how are you?* might, though."

She stopped often as they made their way up and down the rows of vendors. She always gave Court a chance to speak to the merchant first. After he had done so, he seemed content to wait and listen from nearby. She couldn't see those crystal-blue eyes for his sunglasses, but by the tilt of his head he watched what was happening intently.

The crowd thinned at one point and Court stepped beside her. "So, tell me how you came to work at the hospital?"

She bent to pick up a bunch of bananas, said a couple of words to the toothless man then handed him a coin and waited while Court said thank you. "I was working in a hospital ER. One of the traveling nurses told me about the Teligu Hospital and I was intrigued. I needed to make a change and decided to look into coming here."

They moved on to the next vendor.

"Did you always want to work in a developing country?"

A house with children's toys in the yard and a minivan in the drive flashed into her mind. "Not exactly." The words were said slowly. "I've always wanted to be a nurse, though."

He picked up a piece of corn still in its husk from the pile she studied.

"Mealie." Maggie supplied the word.

Court repeated the word. "I wish they were all that easy." Putting the ear back in the pile again, he asked, "Not exactly? What does that mean?"

"Little nosy, aren't you?" She focused on the vegetables on the ground before her.

"Little touchy, aren't you?"

Concentrating on the produce, she tried not to let the hurt show in her eyes. "We all have dreams that don't work out, don't we?"

"Yes."

Maggie glanced at him. The simple word hid more than he let on. Did the aggravating doctor have a secret?

"What's all this for?" He pointed toward the growing amount of food items stuffed into a woven basket she'd brought along.

Relieved at his change of subject, she said, "Supplies for a meal."

"You cook?"

She put a hand on her hip. "Yes, I cook." She mustered as much indignation as she could but tempered the words with a smile.

"I didn't mean to imply…"

"I know what you were implying."

"What I meant was where do you cook?"

"I use the mess hall kitchen on Sunday afternoons. I wish I could use it more often."

"I'm a pretty fair cook myself."

Maggie looked sideways at him in disbelief.

"I am. I learned to make meals on a one-eyed hot plate during medical school. I found cooking an excellent way to release stress after a long day."

With his family background he'd done his own cooking? She would have thought he'd have his own personal chef.

"So who eats these meals you prepare?" Court asked.

She looked at him. "Fishing for an invitation?"

"Could be. I haven't been here long but I already know your cooking has to be better than the usual fare in the mess hall. I'd be willing to assist. I could be your sous chef to earn one?" His grin seemed forced as if he'd not spontaneously shared one in a long time.

Maggie's stomach tightened, flipped and righted in one motion. On Court the grin had been the sexiest she'd ever seen. If he did that and let those incredible eyes come out to play more often, getting an invite would be a sure thing. With a mental shake of her head she said, "We'll see."

Court asked to make her next purchase so he could practice his newfound skill. He did look at her once when the man spoke too fast. As they started back toward the hospital, the crowd thickened again. She'd just suggested they take a longer return route when a commotion drew her attention.

"Missy Maggie, Missy Maggie." Neetie's high-pitched voice filled the air. He rushed at her, wrapping his arms around her legs. Neetie's forward movement propelled her backward. She stumbled and would've been flat on her back if it hadn't been for the strong arm circling her waist.

"Ho, I've got you." Court's breath fluttered warmly against her ear.

The heat of his broad chest against her back reminded her of how long it had been since she'd been held by a man. She'd missed the contact.

Neetie circled to her side and pushed against the back of her legs until he squeezed between her and Court, squealing the entire time, "Help, Missy Maggie, help."

The crowd gave way to a man swinging his hand above his head and shouting. Maggie could understand little of what was being said but she did hear the word *take*.

Court stepped in front of her and assumed a formidable stance. "Stay behind me."

Maggie considered disagreeing with his directive but didn't believe she could take on both Court and the angry man at the same time. Instead, she remained behind and to the side of Court, close enough that she felt him tense as the man approached.

Neetie worked himself between them, half hiding behind her and continuing to chatter. She looked down at the child and said, "Hush, Neetie." He quieted but his eyes remained huge white circles in his dark face.

"Maggie, ask him to stop there, but do not move from behind me, understand?"

She did as instructed, bringing the irate man bearing down on them to a halt.

"Ask him what the problem is," Court said in a tone that had the man looking at him instead of her.

She translated.

"Neetie stole." She looked around Court and Neetie peeped around her legs.

Digging into his pocket, Court brought out a couple of coins and handed them to the man. He used his newfound words of *Thank you* and *Good-bye* and the man left.

Court turned, which brought his mouth to within inches of hers. Her breath caught and held for a moment. He had nice full lips. Her eyes flicked up to meet his. His eyes darkened.

Neetie pushed against their legs, disrupting the moment.

"Let's get out of this crowd," Court said.

Maggie moved the basket up on her arm and took Neetie's hand, and Court clasped her other one. She tried to pull it away but Court held it securely.

"For heaven's sake, Maggie, I just don't want us to get separated in this mob."

All of a sudden she felt silly and accepted the touch of her hand in his. It was no longer necessary for Court to protect her but it still felt nice to have someone look after her for a change.

Reaching the road back to the hospital, Court led them off to the side until they found the shade of a tree. He released her hand and looked down at Neetie.

The boy's eyes widened with fear, and he hopped from side to side.

"Someone should take this child in hand. The boy needs to know he can't steal."

Maggie couldn't disagree and she hoped to be the one receiving responsibility for Neetie soon. She needed to get Neetie's village chief to agree. Would the chief and the village accept her as Neetie's mother? She'd promise to see that Neetie's culture was part of his life. She gave the boy an encouraging smile. Even if she couldn't have a child of her own, her drive to protect remained strong. The pain that had ebbed to a dulled ache over the years sharpened again.

"I'll handle this." She went down on her knees to be at his eye level. "Neetie, what you did was wrong. You should never take what isn't yours."

"But I wanted—"

"That doesn't matter. Court paid for what you took but you'll have to repay him by working it off. I want you to sweep out his bungalow and take out the trash until you have paid him back."

The boy's eyes remained large as he glanced up at Court but he nodded his agreement.

From above her Court said, "Another thing, I want you to be careful about grabbing Missy Maggie. You could've knocked her down. Hurt her. You wouldn't want that, now, would you?"

Neetie gave an earnest negative shake of his head, but still looked terrified. Couldn't Court tell he was scaring the boy? Where had the congenial guy gone who had been with her before Neetie had shown up?

"I'm sorry, Missy Maggie."

She opened her arms and Neetie stepped into them. After giving him a tight hug, she stood and turned to Court. "Thanks for your help back there. I don't know if I could have handled the situation without you."

"I've no doubt you could have." His look met hers. "Maybe I earned that meal after all."

Court had been called in early the next morning to help with an emergency and had been assisting in surgery ever since. He'd had to hustle to get a bite of lunch before going back. He'd not seen Maggie all day. It bothered him not to know where she was and what she was doing. Calling it curiosity and unable to stand it any longer, he'd asked and been told it was her day off.

Bottom line, he missed her. A foreign concept for him. He never let someone interest him enough to miss them. That's what most of his lady friends complained about—he never really cared. He couldn't.

Shaking his head in an effort to remove the idea, Court returned to seeing patients and worked late into the afternoon. He was on his way back to the bungalow when he saw Neetie running up the path. Court couldn't help but be captured by the bundle of energy the young boy presented with his arms flying and sticklike legs pumping. Neetie made him think of the childhood question, "Is that you or are you riding a chicken?"

He sobered. He'd asked Neetie on their return to the hospital from the village how old he was. Neetie had said eight. The age Court had been when his brother had died. The same age that made his heart catch when he cared for a patient. He'd become a pediatrician because of his brother and wanting to help others like him, but in many ways it had been difficult. Especially when his actions caused a child to be disabled. The burden of failure weighed on him like a sack of heavy rocks he never put down.

Neetie slid to a stop out of arm's reach, and looked up at Court with uncertain eyes.

A stab of regret cut through Court. Had he intimidated the boy so much yesterday that he was afraid of him? Court had never meant the boy to fear him.

Neetie pointed down the path from the direction he'd come. "Missy Maggie, help."

Court's heart jerked in his chest and he went down on one knee, meeting the boy at eye level. "What's wrong with Missy Maggie?" The amount of worry those words held surprised Court. When had Maggie started becoming significant enough for him to feel any anxiety over her?

"She in…" Neetie seem to search for the word. He said something in Mamprusi.

"Box?" Court translated.

Neetie gave a vigorous nod and pointed toward the back of the compound.

"A box? What box? Show me."

Neetie scampered down the winding path, and Court followed him at a lope. They went past the bungalows, around a small group of trees and came to what looked like an outdoor storage area. Sitting on the ground were two large metal overseas shipping containers. Neetie pointed into the container with the huge doors flung open. Court looked inside the dark cavern and found the box partially full.

Squinting, he waited while his eyes adjusted from the bright light of the outside to the almost pitch dark inside. He could make out aqua fifty-five gallon plastic drums. They were stacked two high, the top of the second one well above his head. Some of the drums had fallen and were lying at odd angles.

Panic surged through him. Maggie could be seriously hurt. Court stepped into the container. "Maggie?"

"I'm back here."

Relief washed over him, to be replaced by flaming anger. What if he hadn't gotten here in time? What if she'd been too hurt to cry out for help? "Where?" His fear made the word sharp. With a tight chest he took a deep breath and let it out in the hope of slowing his pulse and holding off his irritation at her for being so reckless.

"Straight back."

He turned to Neetie. "You stay here." Court pointed to the ground outside the container, making sure his instructions were clear. Neetie nodded. Court refused to allow another person be injured because he'd failed them. He needed to know that the boy was safe.

With a grunt Court righted a fallen drum. It was heavier than he'd anticipated. What in the world was Maggie doing in here by herself? When he got to her he was tempted to put her over his knee like he would have a disobedient child for scaring him. He continued to move barrels to the side, creating a narrow aisle. "Are you hurt?"

An exasperated sigh came from a few feet in front of him. "Not really."

What the hell did "Not really" mean? "Are you bleeding anywhere?"

"No. Mostly it's my pride that's hurt." Her voice became clearer as he worked his way closer. "I saw a drum marked 'Bandages' up on the top. I knew better than to climb up there and rock it but I did it anyway. I didn't want to take the time to walk all the way to the hospital to get help."

"Yeah, don't do the smart thing. As always, handle it yourself," Court mumbled, while he pushed at another drum with more force than necessary. She was the one everyone turned to for help at the hospital. Amazingly, she always gave it willingly.

"After the first one went they all started falling like dominos. One of the metal clips holding the top closed caught my clothes, and I went down with the barrels."

Her chatter told him that she was more afraid than she'd first let on. Good, she should be. Maybe she'd learned a lesson. He'd reached the deepest part of the fifty-foot box that doubled as a furnace in the late-evening sun. Visibility was dismal at best but he could just make out the top of Maggie's head. He uttered a curse under his breath when he thought of what could have happened. If he'd not seen Neetie…

Court righted the barrels and pushed them to the side, squeezing past them.

Maggie was trapped, half under a barrel. The fury he thought he had under control snapped. "Why're you out here by yourself?" His words cut as sharply as a scalpel. "You should know better."

With a glare, she said, "I do this all the time. It's no big deal. I was doing it before you showed up, and I'll be doing it when you're gone," she snapped.

She had him there. He had no business telling her what she should and shouldn't do. But he still couldn't get the gut-wrenching feeling of what could've happened to her out of his mind. He wiped away the sweat beading heavily on his forehead with the sleeve of his shirt. It had to be over a hundred and ten. "How long have you been in here?"

"All together?"

"Yeah, all together." The sarcasm snapped as bluntly as a dry twig. Yet his professional side kicked in. He needed to keep her talking until he could reach her, so she wouldn't be afraid. She could be seriously injured and, if nothing else, she had to be dehydrated.

"I started working after lunch. A couple of the men were helping me but they got called away."

"How long have you been pinned here?" He enunciated each word as he continued to shift barrels.

"Oh, maybe fifteen minutes."

The temptation to shake her built within him. That fist-size ball of fear he always carried in his gut grew. She sounded so calm about it. It was a wonder she'd not passed out.

Court mumbled a word Neetie didn't need to learn until he was much older. "Maggie, you could've…" He stopped himself from saying more. Getting irate and making her the same wasn't going to help matters. Now was the time to use the cool he'd been so famous for when he'd practiced medicine. He called out the door, "Neetie, go to my bungalow. Get a jug of water and my med bag. It is by the door. Run."

Nettie's rapid prattle of response reached Court's ears. Good, Maggie would need the water when he got her out of here.

Struggling with the bulk of a drum, it made a thump when it rocked on its end. He could see her well now. She sat on the floor of the container, with a drum over her legs, and thankfully one drum supported another so not all the weight rested on Maggie. Her back rested against another barrel.

She looked up at him and with a lift to her chin said, "Of all the places, in all the hospitals, in all the world…"

"Funny, Maggie, real funny." His lips pulled

into a tight line in his desire to stop himself from throttling her. Concern still knotted in his stomach for the risk she'd taken. Outside her being another human and him being a doctor, he couldn't understand way Maggie being injured would matter so much. But it did. "You could've been really hurt."

Court didn't wait for an answer. He considered the drums above them. They looked steady in their places. "Can you hold that one away from you while I pull this one off?"

"Yes."

"On three. One, two, three." Court lifted the barrel, while supporting it with the edge of his foot to prevent it from sliding and falling back onto Maggie. With the drum on its end, he steadied it and moved it out of the way.

Her skirt had bunched up toward her waist, leaving a vast amount of leg exposed and a hint of bright red panties between. As he'd suspected, Maggie had fine legs. Superiorly fine ones.

She swiftly tugged the material down, making herself decent but not totally covering her thighs, before attempting to struggle to her feet. Court reached out to help her. She appeared unhurt but when she put her right foot down, she slumped into him.

"Ooh."

His arm circled her waist, supporting her. "So you did hurt yourself."

"Don't sound so self-satisfied, Doctor. My ankle got caught between two of the drums on the way down, and I pulled it out. It'll be fine by tomorrow."

"I'll have a look at it after we get you out of here."

Court led her through the maze of barrels, assisting the best he could, though they both had to squeeze past drums in some spots. Reaching the open area, he swung Maggie into his arms.

"What're you doing?" she squeaked and shifted against him. "Put me down."

Tightening his hold, he said, "Carrying you." Her body was too hot against him. He had to get her in the shade.

"I can walk."

"Yeah, I saw how well you stood back there. You hang on for a minute, and I'll put you down when we get out of this third circle of hell."

Court felt Maggie's soft laugh against his chest

before he heard it. If he hadn't already been burning up he might have heated more in response to her mirth surrounding him like the sweet smell of spring. He wanted it to last.

He blinked a couple of times before his eyes became accustomed to the brightness of the outside. He found the nearest tree and headed for it, placing Maggie on the ground underneath it. She pushed at the damp curls that had escaped to fall around her face. "I need to fix my hair."

"Leave it be. It looks fine." Kneeling beside her, Court removed her thong from her foot.

"Hey, what're you doing?"

"I'm getting ready to examine you." He lifted her leg and she made a frantic movement to push her skirt down from where it had slid up her leg. "You do realize I have seen a woman's leg before?"

"Yes, I imagine you've seen many."

If he weren't so worried she might be injured, he would've enjoyed the feel of her skin beneath his hand. Running his fingers over the delicate bones of her ankle and halfway up her calf, he found nothing broken.

She jerked her leg from his hand. "I appreciate

your concern but I'm fine." She rotated her ankle a couple of times, before she reached down and rubbed it gently.

Amused at the flustered way she acted, he said, "Seems so."

Her eyes narrowed. "Are you making fun of me, Doc?"

He sat down beside her. He'd learned that when she was ruffled or wanted to put him in his place she used his title instead of his name. "Maybe just a little bit, Nurse. Neetie should be here in a minute with some water, then we'll get you to your bungalow."

"I still have work to do here."

"You're done for the day. Doctor's orders."

"But we need the bandages for clinic tomorrow."

Stubborn woman. "You do know you got off easily. You could've been crushed." He wasn't going to let her go back into the container tonight or any other day by herself ever again. She wouldn't appreciate it but he planned to speak to Dr. Roberts about what had happened. "I'm already tempted to shake you, so don't push me any further."

"Aren't you overreacting a little bit, Doctor?"

Maybe he was, but for a gut-twisting moment while in that box he'd felt that out of control, numbing fear he'd swore never to experience again. He gave her his best pointed look, which had sent many a nurse running, hoping to make it clear he would hold to his threat. Needing to get her mind on something else before they fought, he said, "What's in all these drums anyway?"

"Bandages. Some medical supplies. The envelopes we use to dispense medicine."

"Really?" He wondered about the simple supplies he'd seen used but hadn't thought to ask. During clinic no one had the time to answer unrelated medical questions. "Where do they come from?"

"From the States mostly. Different groups strip old sheets and roll them. They're what we use on the sores we see so many of. Churches send us unused offering envelopes to put meds in. A couple of ladies in Georgia ship us a container about every two years. It's a big help to the hospital."

"Interesting, and impressive. But why are you down here working on your day off?"

"Someone has to do it." Before Court could comment, Neetie arrived with the water and his bag. Standing, Court took the jug, which was almost too large for the boy to handle, bent to one knee and held it to Maggie's lips. She grasped it, guzzling the water. Court supported her back and the jug while she took a long swallow. She'd been more desperate for water than she'd let on. Did she ever complain?

"Slow and easy there. You don't want to overdo it."

Maggie nodded but kept drinking. Finally she'd taken her fill and released the jug. Court offered her a couple pills for pain.

"I don't need those."

"Take them anyway."

She removed the medicine from his hand. In her haste to take them, water ran down her chin and across her chest to wet her thin white shirt. Court could make out the valley between Maggie's breasts and the lacy outline of her bra.

The second she realized the direction his gaze had taken she gave a little yelp, put the jug on the ground and covered herself with her arms.

Court stood and reached for the jug in one movement. He took a long swig of the water but it did little to ease his frustration. It didn't cool his libido. Maggie hid secrets that he'd had a sneak peek at today. No doubt she had other equally fascinating qualities. Ones he refused to let himself explore.

What was happening to him? He had no business being interested in her. Why did Maggie hold such fascination for him?

He'd always enjoyed women. Had all the women friends he wanted, more in some cases. But he never allowed himself to care. Wasn't even sure if he knew how. But for a reason unknown to him this simply dressed, zero makeup, perspiration-soaked, workaholic woman had him wanting to find a spring pool, strip her and spend time showing her the delights between a man and a woman.

Damn. The African sun was already getting to him. Maggie began making movements to stand. Court handed the jug to Neetie and grasped her arm to steady her. She started to pull away but when her ankle gave way, she accepted his help. She hobbled a few yards beside him.

With a resigned sigh, Court leaned down and stretched his arms out in invitation.

"I can make it."

"Yeah, right," Court said in a gruff tone and

scooped her up into his arms. "You and I both know you're going to need to keep off that foot for tonight at least. So shut up and enjoy the ride."

Maggie's indignant huff fluttered his shirt as she lay stiffly in his arms.

"How about some help?"

"What?"

"Put your arm around my neck. Pulling away from me like you are, I might drop you."

She settled an arm around his shoulders and leaned against his chest. She fit against him nicely once she relaxed.

He'd taken special pains to make sure her skirt lay between his bare arms and the smooth skin of her thighs. But he'd not given enough thought to how nice it would be having her body molded to his, to experience her softness against him.

"Neetie," Court called over his shoulder, "run ahead to Missy Maggie's bungalow and be ready to open the door."

The boy gave Court a wide, toothy smile and complied, the bottle bouncing against his leg sloshing water as he ran and Court's bag slung over his small shoulder. Court had to admit he'd been grateful for the boy's help.

Maggie's fingers ruffled the hair at the nape of his neck. "You smell all sweaty." She inhaled dramatically.

What kind of game was she playing? "I'm sure I do."

"But not bad."

She must have heat exhaustion. Or maybe the meds were kicking in. Did she have any idea what kind of flirt she was being? Her actions were so unlike her. He was used to her being standoffish, all business. Court's lips turned up at the corners. She'd hate it tomorrow when she realized how she'd acted.

Maggie's fingers continued their exploration of his hair. She murmured, "You've such silky hair. I've wanted to touch it."

How did he respond? "Thank you" was the only thing that came to mind. Her praise boosted his ego because she'd never given any indication before she'd noticed him personally.

"I need a shower," she said.

Maggie with water trailing down her body was something Court didn't need to be contemplating. His pace increased. He needed to be concerned about getting Maggie to her bungalow and her foot tended. Becoming attached to the charming bit of womanhood in his arms he refused to do.

The heat, being dehydrated, an adrenaline rush with the help of pain pills had made the formidable Maggie quite sweet. The malleable Maggie held too much appeal.

She wiggled closer, running her fingers deeper into his hair. "Thank you," she said in a low whisper, her lips brushing the skin of his neck.

A stab of lust shot through him. He drew in a quick breath. He'd never wanted any woman more than he wanted this sexy bit of mystery.

CHAPTER THREE

MAGGIE woke to the vague memory of Court placing her on the bed. There had been a desperate longing to pull him closer, to sleep.

A rustling noise caught her attention. Neetie sat at the end of her bed.

He grinned. "Mister Doctor say I in charge. You not move until he get back."

"Is that right?"

The bob of Neetie's head almost made her laugh but her own head pounded and her ankle throbbed. She didn't want to do anything to make either worse. Still, she needed a bath. There hadn't been a dry thread on her when Court had helped her out of the container.

Maggie moved to put her feet on the floor.

"No!" Neetie jumped up. "Missy Maggie. You stay. I get in trouble. Mister Doctor say watch. Not get up."

The screen door banged and heavy footsteps

came down the short hallway. Her attention zipped to the doorway. Court entered, carrying a small bag of ice and an ace bandage.

"Hey, there. How're you feeling?"

"Fine." It was a lie but she was sticking with it. Like a light had been flicked on, she remembered how she'd gotten there. Embarrassment added heat to her face. Her gaze left his to focus on a spot at the end of her bed. She gave herself a mental kick for the way she'd acted while in his arms.

"Uh, Neetie, you can go now," Court told the boy without really looking at him.

At Neetie's crestfallen look, she smiled her reassurance. Why wouldn't Court show the boy any real attention? Couldn't he see that Neetie was desperate for some male attention?

Neetie left but with none of the usual childhood exuberance in his walk.

Maggie wanted to beg Neetie to stay. She needed a buffer between her and Court. Being his entire focus made her nervous, out of control. She was *never* nervous, and never let herself be out of control.

"I don't need anyone to take care of me." She moved to sit up but lay back again.

"I'm sure you don't but you're going to get it anyway. We should get this ice on your foot or you won't be able to walk on it tomorrow. Bet you have a headache too."

She disliked a man who was always right. "You're making too much of it. What I need is to be left alone and to get a bath." She swung her legs over the side of the bed.

Court stepped closer but didn't touch her. Maggie stood and put weight on the foot. She gave thanks it didn't ache too much. She straightened, doing her best to pretend it didn't hurt at all. She wanted Court to leave, and he wouldn't if she let on anything different. She'd seen him care for patients, and right now he considered her one. He was a good doctor even if he seemed to dodge caring for the children.

"You can go now." She started toward her closet-size bath.

"I wouldn't count on it." He watched her like a hawk, his body language saying he'd move quickly if she needed him. "You get a shower and then we'll get your foot organized."

"Leave the ice, and I'll see about it." Maggie

closed the door between them. Maybe he'd get the message and be gone when she came out.

She took her shower without any mishaps but she'd forgotten to get any clean clothes. Wrapping a towel loosely about her, her foot starting to throb, she opened the door a crack. Surely Court had understood her dismissal.

"Forget something?" He leaned against the cinder-block wall. Hooked to the end of his crooked index finger hung one of her paper-thin nightgowns.

"How dare you? You went through my clothes."

His lips broadened into a full-fledged smile. "You left me no choice. It was that or you'd come out naked." His voice dropped lower and his attention moved downward, then up again. "I wouldn't have objected but it's time you got off your foot. I was trying to expedite things."

Maggie released a disgusted puff of air.

"I promise it won't happen again," he said with a glint in his eye that preventing her from believing him. Maggie snatched her gown off his finger. "You can leave now." She tried to slam the door in his face but the flimsy plywood didn't provide the effect she had hoped for.

Court's deep baritone chuckle said the effort had been noticed. "You're starting to sound like a broken record."

"It would be nice if someone would listen," she murmured as she pulled on her gown.

She came out of the bath, sighing in relief not to see Court. At least he'd finally done something she asked. Taking the few steps to her bed was more difficult than she'd imagined. Her ankle hurt like the devil.

But she had to take care of her hair. That was one demand her dad had made that she couldn't let go of. "You must keep your hair out of your face." She'd dry it the best she could with the towel then comb it out.

Maggie pulled the comb through a section of hair. She'd been relieved when Neetie and then Court had shown up. For a while, she'd feared she'd gotten herself into a situation she wasn't going to recover from easily. It had been uncomfortable to hear Court reprimand her about being in the container alone but she knew he was right.

"Hey, can't the hairdo wait? You need to get your foot up," Court said as he slid something across her bedside table. He took the comb from her. "Foot up. Ice pack on."

She curled her upper lip. "You're back?" It came out more like a groan than a real complaint. Why wouldn't he just leave her alone?

He lifted her leg.

"What're you doing?"

"If you're not going to see about your foot, I will."

She scooted back. He put her foot on a pillow and placed the ice bag across the ankle.

"You couldn't walk to the mess hall for dinner so I had no choice but to see that you got some food."

"Thanks. That's very gracious of you," she said reluctantly. "Leave it and I'll eat in a little while." She looked at the plate covered with a napkin on a cookie sheet, and her mouth quirked in question.

"I know but the guys were busy and didn't have time to find me a tray. I saw the pan and thought it would work."

She couldn't squelch her mirth. The Boston socialite serving dinner on a cookie sheet in an African hut. It had to be a first. "If I eat, will you leave?" She pushed herself into a sitting position, making sure to cover her chest with the sheet. Court set a plate on the table, laid the pan across her lap and placed her drink close at hand. Maggie lifted the napkin to find chicken, vegetables and a nice-size piece of cake. He pulled a straight chair close, angling it so he faced her.

"What're you doing now?"

He picked up the plate and sat. "I'm hungry. I might as well join you because I'd have to come back and get your dishes anyway." He forked corn into his mouth like he often took his meals in a woman's bedroom.

Was arguing with him worth the breath? He would do as he pleased, no matter what she said. That much she had learned about him.

"I can hear you thinking. Eat."

Despite what Maggie had imagined, they had a comfortable meal, even though neither spoke. When she'd finished he took her plate. Exhausted, she slid down into the bed. Her eyelids drooped. It had been her experience that if she disappointed men enough, they didn't bother to stay around long enough to have a chance to take care of her.

Before sleep took her she heard, "Good night, Magnificent Missy Maggie."

* * *

All day Court and Maggie had been working at the clinic. She'd helped him with cases since early morning and still couldn't get her nerve up to ask him to dinner the next evening. She hated to admit it but she owed Court, and being indebted to him went against the grain. She'd made a practice of not letting it happen, even took pride in being self-sufficient.

With recent events, which had been out of her control somewhat, she'd managed to become beholden to the first guy who'd held her notice in a long time. Maggie sighed. Very much the wrong guy. They had no future. He was here for another week and then he'd be gone, never to return, like all the others. Plus, they couldn't agree on the financial help the hospital needed. That point she couldn't give on. Still, she should show her thanks. Her parents had brought her up to be polite, and she would be so even if being around Court made her uncomfortable in ways she didn't like to admit to. She couldn't put it off any longer. They'd seen the last patient and Court finished up by making notes in the patient's log book. She spent time putting the clinic in order for the next day but did more than necessary. It was now or never.

Marshaling her courage, Maggie took a deep breath and said, "Uh, Court…"

He looked at her, his brows raised in question. With exhaustion from a long day showing on his face and evening shadow covering his jaw, he was still the best-looking man she'd ever seen. Her fingers twitched with the urge to push his hair off his forehead and massage his temples.

"I wanted to say thank you for seeing about the bandages."

She'd woke that morning to find her foot stiff and a little sore but not so much so she couldn't perform her duties. She approached Dr. Roberts at breakfast to say there were still some bandages in the container needing to be retrieved. Dr. Roberts informed her it had already been taken care of. At what had to be her look of shock he said, "Dr. Armstrong and a few of the men saw to it earlier. And, Maggie, he also told me what happened yesterday. I want you to be more careful in the future. Don't go in the containers by yourself. Much too dangerous." It miffed her that Court had spoken to her superior. She'd been on her own for years and didn't need him going behind her back to Dr. Roberts. He meant well but she didn't like him messing in her business. But despite being aggravated at Court, she still appreciated his help. The bandages were needed in clinic.

"You're welcome." His attention returned to the log.

"Court…"

"Yes?" he said, his mouth narrowing.

Why was she having such a hard time asking him such a simple question? She wasn't the nervous ninny type. She had to get a grip.

"I'd like to say thank you for seeing about the bandages, seeing about me yesterday and helping Neetie out the other day in the market." Gracious, she had a long list. How had he managed to become so tangled in her life in such a short time?

He shrugged. "Not a problem."

Court looked away before she blurted out, "Would you like to come to dinner tomorrow night? I'm cooking."

He sat straighter. She had his complete attention. His lips lifted at the corners, spread wider, and his summer-blue eyes twinkled. "Why, Missy Maggie, I'd love to come to dinner."

Darn him, he was making fun of her nervous-ness but with such charm she didn't mind. In fact, having him give her that sexy smile was worth being made fun of. Maybe him leaving in a little over a week was a good idea. Sooner might be better.

"Good, I'll expect you at six." Maggie left with the sound of his warm chuckle filling the space between them.

Court contemplated Maggie's invitation to dinner as he made his way to the mess hall. More than one woman had asked him out but he'd never had one who so obviously hated doing so. If she hadn't felt the need to thank him in some way, he had no doubt she wouldn't have.

He'd looked forward to their meal all day. She never ceased to surprise him, from her evident love for the Mamprusi she helped, to the respect of the people she worked with, to her over-the-top determination to make a difference. Even if she had to do it all by herself. But the woman needed a keeper. Full time. Who was going to get her out of scraps when he left?

He was headed someplace he didn't need to go.

She had been fine before he'd arrived and she would be fine after he left. Maggie wasn't his to worry about. No one was, and he liked it that way. Wanted it that way. If he didn't let her become important to him, he didn't have to worry about failing her or, worse, feeling the pain of losing her.

The gentle sound of humming filled the mess hall. While he crossed the dining area toward the kitchen the humming turned into a burst of words from a rock-and-roll song he recognized but couldn't put a name to. Maggie had a nice voice. Not the first thing he'd found *nice* about Maggie over the past few days.

He'd shown up early. For some reason he couldn't fathom, he'd been drawn to the mess hall all afternoon. He'd even gone through all the wards, seeking a chore to help him stall for time. It had been no lie when he'd told Maggie he enjoyed cooking. If she was good enough to cook for him, he could at least be nice enough to help out. He'd use that excuse anyway. Helping her would also give him a chance to learn more about life in Ghana. Something the hurried schedule in clinic didn't allow. Plus, it might be a good stress reliever—something he not had much of in the past few months.

He stepped into the kitchen, stopped cold and shot to hot.

Maggie's back was to him and her hips were swaying to the beat of the music. Court's stomach contracted like he'd been gut-punched. His pulse pounded in his ears. She wore shorts. Not an extremely tall woman, she still had the longest, shapeliest, sexiest legs he'd ever seen.

Court eyes fixed on the muscled but gently rounded thighs before moving down past the crevice behind her knees to the sloping arch of her calves. Had it just been the day before yesterday when he'd run his hands over her smooth skin? His gaze paused at her thin-boned ankles and her bare feet, before taking his time retracing his previous path of sight back up her leg.

He gulped. Oh, yes, he was a leg man all right, and Maggie had an outstanding pair. What would it be like to have one of those wrapped around him in bed? His body hardened at the thought.

Mercy, he was losing it. Had he been out in the heat too long?

Had her keeping her legs hidden so well under

skirts made them even more appealing? Was it because they were forbidden, or because they were Maggie's? He wanted to believe the former true but he wouldn't bet on it. He knew lust when he felt it. He was a red-blooded male and he appreciated women.

But Maggie was the type of woman who led with her heart. He'd seen it more than once as she cared for patients during clinic and while talking to Neetie. His feelings were securely vaulted away. He didn't do relationships, and he didn't see Maggie as a one-night-stand type.

The CD player she sang along with stopped. She must have heard a movement because she chose that moment to turn. Her mouth formed an O, and her eyes widened.

The knife she held fell to the floor with a tinkle of stainless steel. Their gazes held, while the knife rattled to a stop on the cement floor. Sexual awareness hung in the air like a cotton-candy-thick fog.

Court watched her swallow, wishing he could trace the subtle movement with a tip of his finger.

He had to get a hold on his desire or he'd have her on the counter in no time. Maggie deserved better. *Yeah, right. Like she would allow him to touch her.* She'd made it clear a number of times that she was off-limits. Shifting his weight to make the evidence of his interest less obvious in his cargo shorts, he said, "Maggie, you have shorts on."

His high-priced Boston education, and years of fancy words in medical school had certainly disappeared from his vocabulary. He sounded like a teenage boy who'd just realized girls came in more varieties than sisters.

She raised an eyebrow and laughed. "Yes, I have shorts on. Thanks for letting me know."

It had been a long time since someone had had the chutzpah to make fun of him. Why did Maggie finding humor at his expense not bother him? He couldn't help but join in her laughter. Her pure notes swirled around his deep, rougher tone and became one.

He reached down at the same time she did to pick up the knife. His hand skimmed hers. Time stopped then surged forward. Maggie pulled her hand back and stepped away. He tossed the knife into the sink. Turning round, he found Maggie starting to wrap a piece of material around her waist.

"You don't have to cover up on my account."

She tossed him a look that said *Stop now before you go too far* as she finished putting on her skirt. "Why're you here? I wasn't expecting you for another hour or so."

"I'm your sous chef. Reporting for duty." He gave her a small military salute.

"Yeah, right. You taking orders. I don't see that happening."

"Ouch. That hurt. Please, chef, give me a try. I might surprise you."

The twinkle in his eyes and the twist of his lips made her wonder if the statement might have a double meaning. She had no intention of letting this fly-in, fly-out doctor take her heart with him when he left. But she couldn't push him too far away. She needed to at least be friendly, so she could convince him the hospital needed the foundation's support.

Everyone understood the mess hall was her sanctuary on Sunday evenings and they wouldn't enter. Either Court hadn't heard or he didn't care. Most likely didn't care, since he did as he saw fit.

She'd looked forward to this time of solitude in her week. But would it be so bad to share it with Court just one time? Except for her heart rate rising, temperature over the top and melting-in-her-center awareness of him. Still, it felt gratifying to have an attractive man's attention. Something she hadn't realized she'd missed.

"Okay, I'm going to give you a shot." She pointed a finger at him, "But you remember who gives the orders here, Doctor."

He went into the snappy salute again. "Yes, ma'am."

She laughed. He made her do that often, among other things. "All right, your first job is to cut up these vegetables. Knife and cutting board are in the right-hand drawer on the end." She pointed down the stainless-steel counter.

They worked without speaking. Maggie was aware with every fiber in her that Court stood nearby, conscious of his slightest movement. Only through great willpower did she manage not to glance at him every thirty seconds. She didn't have the solitude she generally craved but still she found she liked have him close.

What she should be doing instead of mooning over Court was taking the opportunity to get his impressions of the hospital. He wasn't going to be here much longer and she needed to convince him the hospital deserved the funding of the Armstrong Foundation.

The chopping suddenly stopped. He glanced at her. She'd been caught staring. She hoped that the heat of the kitchen covered the heat that touched her cheeks.

"Court, I was wondering what you thought about the work we do at the hospital." She tried to make the question sound casual.

He put down the knife he'd been using to cut the vegetables and leaned his hip against the counter. "There's good work being done here, and I see the need in a number of areas. I wish there could be more prevention education being done. The hospital sees too many cases where earlier intervention would help greatly. Keep infections from getting out of hand. Like your friend's leg."

"I tried—"

Court reached out, his touch to her arm reassuring. Maggie turned back to the pot on the range. She could still feel his fingers on her skin even though he'd removed his hand.

"Maggie, you shouldn't feel guilty. You did everything you could to get her to come to the hospital. You can't force people to be who they're not."

She concentrated on stirring while she adjusted to the prick of old pain that caught her unawares. It sounded like Court knew that firsthand. Her ex-fiancé had more than proven that statement true when he'd broken off their engagement. He'd been brought up to believe his virility meant that he would produce a male child. When she'd lost the ability to conceive, he'd waited until she'd gotten out of the hospital before he called the wedding off. She was no longer perfect.

"Also, I see the need to set up some kind of relationship between a secondary hospital and this one," Court said, standing too close for her comfort. "Where patients can receive more advanced help in a shorter amount of time. A new pediatric ward needs to be built, or at least added on to the established one."

Unsure if it was the right thing to ask, she couldn't stop herself. She had to know. "Are you reconsidering the grant application?" She turned around and found herself toe to toe to him.

Court's eyes bored into hers. "I'm still unsure."

She had the funny thought that they were no longer talking about the same thing. *He wants to kiss me.* "Why not?" she said breathlessly, then shook her head, trying to remember what they were really talking about. "You've seen the needs here. You even recognize them. What else do you have to know?"

She watched indecision fill his amazing eyes, then the shutters closing before he backed away. "Maggie," he said with a roughness to his voice, "I'm the CEO. I can offer an opinion, if I wish to, but a committee makes the final decision on where the funds are allocated."

"Why?" Maggie couldn't keep her disappointment out of her voice. Was it because he didn't kiss her or from his answer? The heat she felt from his look still warmed her.

He went back to chopping the vegetables with more force than necessary. "Because I still need more time to make an adequate evaluation."

Again, were they talking about the same thing? "For crying out loud, what more could we do to prove the need? Have an epidemic?"

"I won't be bullied on this, Maggie. I haven't

said no, I've just said wait." His tone implied that would be the end of the discussion.

She didn't understand his attitude about the grant and she missed their earlier camaraderie that had been there between them for those precious moments. She wanted it back. Returning to preparing a pan for the meat with shaking hands, she listened to the rhythm of his chopping.

"Okay, is this it? Sure seems like plenty to me." By the sound of his voice the old Court had returned. He moved so she could see the chopping board.

She wished she could say yes but old habits died hard. "Could you make them a little more uniform in size?"

He looked at her in disbelief but nodded anyway. "Yes, chief."

"Then you could peel potatoes."

"What? Am I in the army now?"

She leaned a hip against the counter and crossed a foot over the other, her toe pointed on the floor. "You don't plan to remain my sous chef for long, do you?"

"I didn't know you were going to be such a particular taskmaster. Is there any place you don't like being the boss? Where are the potatoes?"

Maggie pointed to the basket under the counter. "All of them?"

Maggie nodded. "There'll be eight of us eating." She returned to the fruit glaze she'd been preparing to top the dessert. She tied on an apron after some of the sticky syrup splashed on her.

The CD started to play again after finishing a set. She and Court softly sang along while they worked. Despite their previous tension, Maggie couldn't remember the last time she'd enjoyed preparing a meal so much. Court carried a bowl of potatoes over to her.

"Are these the right size?" he teased.

She resisted the strong urge to ask him to make them smaller but instead she said, "They're fine." She moved but not quickly enough and Court brushed up against her as he dumped the potatoes into the roasting pan she'd oiled. Once again the tension sparked and flashed in the air between them.

Court set the bowl on the counter, then slid a hand around her waist, pulling her against his solid body. Cupping her face, he gently brushed the pad of his thumb across the apple of her cheek. "I believe I will," he said in a deep, sandpapery voice.

"Wha—?"

"Kiss the cook," he whispered, before his lips touched hers briefly, retreated and returned to rest firmly against hers. His mouth felt cool, confident and completely in control. He tasted divine.

He didn't demand a response but she couldn't resist the desire to lean into him. Fireworks went off inside her. Mercy, the man could kiss.

He murmured, "You taste good."

She shivered. Did an astronaut feel the same when he broke out of the earth's gravity? Weightless, suspended, out of control?

The slap of the outside door broke their self-absorbed cocoon. Court had stepped away by the time one of the nurses entered the kitchen.

With her blood humming like an express train and her body warm as if she'd stepped out of a sauna, Maggie looked down at the front of the apron to find the faint words *Kiss the Cook* printed on it. With a quick movement, she turned back to the stove and spoke over her shoulder. "Hey, dinner should be ready in a few minutes. Would you mind setting the table? There'll be eight of us."

"Sure, I'll be glad to." Lisa turned and headed back into the dining area. Another slap of the double screen door brought a call of, "Missy Maggie."

"In here, Neetie." She smiled as the boy bounced into the kitchen area. "Hungry?"

"Yeah."

"Court, would you dish up Neetie a plate of food?" She might have missed Court's stricken look if she hadn't glanced at him.

"Why don't you let me see about that?" He came over and took the spoon from her hand. "While you get Neetie his dinner."

Left no choice, Maggie moved out of the way. What was wrong with him? Did he not like children or Neetie in particular? She couldn't understand how he'd managed to be a children's doctor and not like children. During clinic she'd noticed he'd shied away from the children and offered to take the older patients, directing the mothers with youngsters to one of the other doctors.

After she'd hurt her foot Court and Neetie had seemed to be a little more at ease with each other. She loved children and couldn't imagine anyone else not liking them too. Especially if you were a children's doctor.

She said, "Sure, I'll take care of him," even as she wondered at the shadowed look filling Court's eyes.

There had been those few tense moments like the one when he'd refused to see about Neetie, but despite those the evening had been exceptional, Court thought. One of the nicest he'd had in a long time. He'd not eaten a more delicious meal or enjoyed a more lively discussion in any fine home or restaurant than he'd experienced with this group of hard-working, dedicated people.

Finished with eating, they all pushed their chairs back and began telling stories that made them more than coworkers. Their jobs were difficult and their living conditions were little above primitive but they knew how to appreciate downtime. They were a family and for once in his life he knew what it felt like to be a member, not an outsider. It was nice.

Watching Maggie toss her head back and laugh made a shot of unadulterated pleasure flow through him like warm caramel over a fresh-baked cake. Pure heaven. Her laugh reminded him of a girl giggling but with the maturity of a woman who knew herself and her place in the world. The combination intrigued him.

After an hour or so Dr. Roberts cleared his throat, drawing everyone's attention. "I hate to break up the party but I have to check on a patient in the ward. Before I go, Doctors..." he looked at Court and John "...we need to decide who's going to handle the clinics in the villages with Maggie and Bee. Court, would you mind going?"

"There are a large number of children due for check-ups. Maybe Court would rather not have to do so much child care," Maggie suggested, looking at him as if challenging him to refuse to go.

Court felt a spasm of unease at the thought of handling the child care by himself but he refused to let that show. He took a deep breath and said, "I'd like to see a village." Maggie's crestfallen look gave him some satisfaction, even if it didn't ease his apprehension. Surely there would be no cases worse in the village than the kind of thing he'd already seen in the past few days. "It would give me a better understanding of the kind of work the hospital is doing with the out-lying clinics."

"But—"

"Then it's settled," Dr. Roberts said, cutting off what Court knew would be Maggie's objection. Court had fully expected Maggie to start building barriers after their heated kiss but he'd not thought she would be so obviously against working with him. "Great. Sounds like a plan.

"When do we leave?"

"Five a.m.," Maggie stated.

"O-kay. I'll be ready."

"Court, I'll leave you in Maggie's and Bee's ca-pable hands," Dr. Roberts said. "Maggie, check in with me before you leave in case I have any last-minute instructions."

"Will do," Maggie said, and started stacking dishes.

"And by the way, great meal. Thanks," Dr. Roberts announced, and everyone agreed.

"Don't worry about the washing-up," Jill said. "You probably need to get stuff together. You cooked, we'll clean." She looked pointedly at the others around the table.

"Great. Thanks, everyone." Maggie waved over her head before heading toward the door.

"Wait a minute, would you? I need to talk to you," Court called, hurrying after her. At the grumbles behind him, he called over his shoulder, "Hey, I helped cook."

Maggie had made it out the door before he reached her side. "Maggie, wait up. I need to know what supplies I should see about or if there's anything else I need to do before tomorrow morning."

"Nothing special. The supplies are already boxed and ready to load. The boys will have them in the truck and tied down for us before it's time to leave. Have your personal med bag well stocked, get some rest and be prepared to work long hours."

"How long will we be gone?"

"Four to five days." She said the words matter-of-factly but her voice vibrated with a hint of excitement.

"You're looking forward to this trip, aren't you?"

"Yes. This is my favorite village. Neetie's from there. He'll be going with us. If you don't mind, I'll answer all your other questions tomorrow. Take my word for it—we'll have plenty of time to talk. It's a long drive." She turned and headed toward the hospital building.

Court couldn't remember being so prettily dismissed in quite some time.

The stars were still bright in the night sky when Maggie came round the corner of the motor-pool building. The soft silence and dim light from the security light surrounded her. She expected to see the drab green military surplus truck loaded and ready to go but surprise filled her when she saw the tall, lanky form of Court leaning against it.

He wore an outfit that reminded her of Indiana Jones, right up to the hat tipped rakishly on his handsome head. Maggie's heart leaped. An unexpected desire to knock his hat off and kiss him good-morning washed over her. Ho, she shouldn't have those kinds of thoughts. She was stuck with the high-handed, arrogant man for the next few days and this wasn't some African vacation for the wealthy.

"Mornin', Maggie."

She almost groaned at the sound of his deep voice passing through those lips, the thoughts of which had kept her awake much of the night.

Taking a deep fortifying breath, she said, "Let me check with Dr. Roberts, find Bee and Neetie, and we'll be off."

"Neetie's asleep in the back. Roberts said to tell you he had to go into surgery and Bee won't be going. One of the other nurses is sick, and Roberts said he can't spare her. So it's just you and me," he teased. "And Neetie, of course. I'll drive."

She debated with him about driving because he didn't know the way to the village but he said, "I can take directions. I'm a quick learner."

She hated to admit it, but he did catch on quickly. He had a good ear for language and had picked up enough Mamprusi to carry on a pleasant conversation with the locals. On top of that, she'd not heard him complain about working under time pressure or the constraints of the hospital's limited abilities. Grudgingly, she acknowledged Court had adjusted well to living in Ghana. She made a face under the cover of darkness. "Take the road north out of town."

They left the buildings of the compound behind and Maggie rested her head against the truck door, taking advantage of the unexpected opportunity to get some sleep. Closing her eyes, she couldn't prevent the memory of Court's lips on hers from slipping in.

Was he having as much trouble recovering from their kiss as she was?

CHAPTER FOUR

MAGGIE woke with a start. The bump and shudder of the truck after the tire hit an extra-deep rut in the dry road bed knocked her head against the window.

She glanced at Court. The dawning light put his profile in sharp relief. She allowed herself a few seconds to appreciate the way his hair fell over his forehead, the set of his generous mouth and the jut of his firm jaw. She would have spent more time admiring his classically handsome good looks but she refused to let her interest show.

The sun was creeping into the sky. Court had been driving for hours. She shouldn't feel sorry for him; it had been his choice and at his insistence. He'd climbed into the cab, leaving her no alternative but to go round to the passenger side. She didn't mind being driven but she did mind the high-handed way he gone about it.

Court turned his head and his pale blue gaze

met hers for a flicker of a second before her lids dropped.

"I know you're awake," he said just above a whisper, "because I've been listening to those delicate little sounds you make for the past few hours."

Maggie twisted in her seat and glared. "Are you implying I snore?"

"Oh, no. These are more like little noises of pleasure. As if you were dreaming of something delightful."

Unaccustomed heat crept into her face. Oh, man, she'd been thinking of his kiss as she'd gone to sleep. A change of subject was needed. She looked through the dusty windshield to the expanse of monochromatic land before them. One lone tree stood off in the distance. "You've made good time."

"I thought so but it's hard to tell in this environment. It all looks the same."

"It does until you've been here for a while. Then each area takes on its own personality. Even though it changes often, some things never change. Like that tree out there. It has become a marker, a guide to all who travel along this way."

"What happens when it dies?"

"Then another marker will be chosen." She pointed off to the left. "The small rocky rise will always be there. We'll need to stay to the right of it."

"You love this place, don't you?"

"I do. These people need me."

Court let the statement sink in. She had no idea she'd told him something significant about herself. Strong, independent Maggie needed to be needed. That was something he could understand. Having felt on the outside, with an invisible barrier between him and the rest of his family, he knew the desire well.

"Do you see yourself always living here?"

"Yes."

He glanced at her, brow raised. "You don't want to marry? Have kids?" She looked away, as if she didn't want him to see her face. He couldn't image Maggie not wanting children. They seemed to gravitate to her during clinics. More than once he had been envious of her ease with them. Something he had lost and didn't know if he would ever get back.

"No, the kids like Neetie are my children. In

fact, I plan to ask the chief if I may adopt Neetie on this trip. Anyway, the majority of the men I meet have no interest in living here. This is my home now."

The wiry-haired head of Neetie popping between them prevented Court from asking another question.

"We stop soon?" Neetie asked.

Giving him an affectionate rub of his head, Maggie answered, "When we get to the Remember Tree we'll stop. It isn't far ahead."

Maggie had a knack with children. She'd make a magnificent mother to Neetie. There would be no wife or child in his future. He had nothing to give, or if he did he refused to. Opening himself to the possibility also exposed him to pain and misery. He couldn't give a family what they needed most—his unguarded heart. "Remember Tree?" Court asked.

"Yeah. That one we were just talking about."

"Why Remember Tree?"

"Because it is the one Neetie uses to remember how to get home." She smiled back at Neetie.

"I still don't get it."

"When Neetie left to go to school in Teligu

he was afraid he wouldn't remember how to get home. We picked out landmarks along the way so that he would know his way back to his village. So this tree became the Remember Tree."

"I see," Court said quietly. Remembering was something they weren't allowed to do in his family. Lyland, his twin brother, was never mentioned. Maybe if his parents would let themselves, let him, remember, Court could find his way back to his family. Unlike Neetie, Court still searched for his Remember Tree.

By the time they had reached the tree it was approaching noon and the temperature was nudging a hundred. Maggie instructed Court to pull the truck well under the tree to protect them from the heat as much as possible.

Pulling a box out of the backseat, Maggie said, "We'll eat on the tailgate."

Neetie climbed into the back of the truck, while Court and Maggie stood and ate their sandwiches.

"How often do you make this trek out to the village?" Court asked between bites of sandwich.

Maggie picked up a piece of fruit. "Usually once a quarter, but more often if necessary."

"How do you know if you need to go more often?"

"This is the main trek to the south so someone is always coming through from this direction. They'll stop and tell us if we're needed."

"Is the village much farther?"

"We should reach it before nightfall."

"Really? That much farther?"

"It takes two days in the rainy season but in the dry it's one long day. Tired already? Want me to drive?"

"No. I'm good."

Maggie started packing the remaining food into the box. "Neetie, would you get the water jug for me? You can show Mister Doctor how we take a shower."

The boy scrambled over the side of the truck and returned with a large container of water, handing it to her. At Court's questioning look, she smiled.

"Shower?" he asked. "Sounds interesting."

The pink in her cheeks wasn't just from the heat. He sure enjoyed teasing her. She always had such a pretty reaction to it.

"It isn't that kind of shower. We'll easily dehydrate in this heat, especially riding in a closed truck. We need to counteract that by wetting ourselves down."

Maggie poured water over Neetie's head. With the bottle empty, she went to the cooler on the side of the truck and refilled it. She upended the bottle over her hair, face and across her shoulders. It gradually soaked her navy T-shirt.

Court watched with rapt attention as wetness continued to flow across the fullness of her pert, round breasts, defining them. His mouth turned dry but not from the sweltering heat. He fervently wished her T-shirt was white. He swallowed. Did the woman have any idea what she was doing to him? Snarling low in his throat, Court put his back to Neetie before the boy got a lesson in the birds and the bees.

Maggie glanced at Court, and away. Her eyes returned and widened. Her mouth formed an O.

"Hand me that bottle and get Neetie in the truck. I'll be there in a minute."

"But—"

"Damn it, Maggie, just this once, do as I say without an argument."

Maggie knew desire. She'd experienced it. She'd

had boyfriends, a fiancé, but never had a man respond to her so swiftly and visibly as Court had.

At his intense stare, her nipples had puckered and her breasts had grown heavy. A river of heat had flowed through her body and pooled low, creating a throbbing that still beat. A slight tremble shook her body.

The corners of her mouth lifted. There was a sweet giddiness to having sexual power over a big strapping man. She liked it that she could stir Court so. But something told her not to push him too far or he'd turn and bite, leaving her hurting.

Neetie had settled in the backseat by the time Court opened the driver's door.

"I'll be glad to drive," she said in as even a tone as she could muster with her nerves in a jumble.

"I've got it."

"Okay, if that's the way you want it."

He gave her a piercing look. "You have no *real* idea what I want."

Hours later, with the sky turning red on the horizon, she could see the village in the distance. Neetie with his skinny arm stretched between them squealed, "The kissing well."

"And that is?" Court remarked.

"It's where his mother last kissed him goodbye."
She'd said the words so softly he'd glanced at her.

"Forever?" he said the word quietly.

"Yes, forever." She gave a little nod, wondering
at the shadows in his eyes before he turned away.

Maggie's heart rate always picked up from excitement when she entered the village. Court drove
along the path as she directed him between mud-
brick huts with their pointed roofs.

"That's a mighty big smile on your face," Court
commented, with a hint of teasing.

"Yeah, I love coming here. These villagers have
a better sense of what life is about than most people I know. Here life is hard, and many die young,
but they understand the value of laughing and lov-
ing. They love despite it all. They'll party tonight
because we have arrived."

She sensed more than saw him tense. Had something she'd said bothered him? "Don't worry, you
won't be expected to dance unless the chief asks."

"Thanks. I happen to be a good dancer."

"Make a right. The chief's huts are those sitting
off by themselves."

"Huts?"

"Yes, huts." She turned and grinned. "The one in the center is the chief's and the others surrounding it are his wives'."

Court's brow rose in a charming manner, making Maggie's stomach dip. "As in more than one?"

She chuckled, "As in ten, and he's still a fairly young man."

"I'm impressed. Not even one wife sounds like a good plan to me, much less ten."

"Not man enough to handle it, Doctor?" she quipped.

"Questioning my virility? No, it's all the other stuff that comes along with being a husband I'm not comfortable with. I assure you—" he looked her straight in the eye "—I can handle the love-making part with no trouble."

Maggie's stomach flittered, and she warmed all over. She had no doubt he could.

Thankfully she was saved by the children and a few young adults running up to the truck to greet them. In the backseat, Neetie chattered loudly and non-stop in his excitement to be home.

As soon as the truck stopped, Neetie was off and running. Court climbed out and came round to stand beside her. She hugged a number of the children and spoke to others, explaining that Court was the doctor who had come to help them. Maggie noticed a group of young women huddled together. They were looking at Court and whispering. Each of those women would no doubt have some prefabricated illness by tomorrow's clinic. Maggie couldn't blame them. Court was a fine-looking man.

In order to be heard over the noise of everyone talking at once, Court leaned over and spoke to her. "They seem to be glad to see us."

"They are. A visitor is rare and medical help even rarer. We need to see the chief and pay our respects."

Maggie led the way to the largest hut. A tall, lean man with a bright but toothless smile waited for them. Maggie dipped her head to acknowledge his position as leader and then turned to Court, pleased to find that he had followed her lead. Maggie explained to the chief who Court was and why he was there.

When she stopped talking Court said, "Tell him I am pleased to be in his village and look forward to meeting his people."

Maggie did as asked. The two men sized each other up and then both nodded to each other again.

"Welcome, Miss Maggie," the chief said. "You have brought good medicine to us again."

"Do you want us to hold clinic in the same place as before?"

"Yes. And one of my wives will be staying with me so you stay in her hut." He looked at her and then at Court.

Her heart fluttered and then found its rhythm again. She said thank you and turned to leave. "Thank you for your hospitality. And your wife's," Maggie said, with more sincerity than she felt.

When she and Court were outside he asked, "What did he say? I can tell by the look on your face you're not pleased."

Maggie opened the truck door and then looked at him. "We'll be sharing one of his wife's huts as our quarters while we're here."

"Really? There's not another option? Another hut where I could stay?"

"I don't like it any better than you do but I can't offend the chief by complaining about the arrangements. And neither can you. This isn't a fancy hotel where you can just get another room if you're not pleased with the one you have."

She started climbing into the truck. Surely they could survive a few nights in a hut alone. Court hadn't made a move to touch her since their kiss in the mess hall anyway.

The chief had followed them out and Neetie skidded up to him. "I show."

The chief nodded, his smile indulgent. "Come eat tonight," he called to Maggie and Court.

Neetie climbed into the truck and started throwing the bags out. Court walked over and helped, hefted hers over his shoulder along with his. "Lead the way, Neetie."

Maggie fell in behind the two of them. Neetie led them to the hut the farthest out of the village. Court pushed back the heavy blanket that served as a door. Neetie ducked under Court's arm and entered. Court continued to hold it, allowing her to enter before him. "Home, sweet home," he mumbled as she passed.

Maggie groaned. Court wasn't going to make this easy.

Neetie dropped the bags he carried and left before Court made it into the hut. "Bye," he said over his shoulder.

Maggie laughed, and called after him. "Have a good time with your cousins."

She glanced at Court. He was surveying the hut with its pounded dirt floor and fire pit in the middle.

"Not the fancy five-star hotels you're probably used to, is it?" Her voice held more humor than sarcasm.

"This's pretty primitive."

"Ready to go home, Doctor? This is a million-dollar-home in this village. Did you expect room service?"

"I did not, but more than a dirt floor I did expect. Where're the beds?"

Maggie pointed to the mat on the floor. She couldn't control the quirk on her lips. "You do know if there had been any other way I would've gotten us out of this. But in this village in particular, the chief's word is law. No one argues with him."

"Well, if it'll make you feel any better, I'll stay on my side of the circle if you stay on yours." He picked up his duffel bag and dropped it beside the woven mat on the floor across from where she stood.

"I don't think it'll be a problem," Maggie said, pushing her bag with a foot toward the other mat to put at least six feet between them.

"Before it gets dark, why don't you show me where we'll be holding clinic?"

"Sure. But let's stop by the truck and get a flashlight before we head over there."

They were making their way to the other side of the village when Court said, "So, tell me about Neetie's family."

"There isn't much to tell. He doesn't have any."

"But you said he was playing with his cousins," Court said as they weaved through the huts.

"He is but he has no brothers or sisters. His father was killed in an accident and his mother died during an epidemic a few years back."

"So who is responsible for him?"

"No one person. But I hope to change that. The village does what they can but taking someone extra into their home can mean major hardship." She stopped and turned to him. "These people are poor and one more mouth to feed can be one too many."

"So how did Neetie end up at the compound?"

"He had a bad wound that needed care. He was bright—"

"And you took him under your wing and he stayed." It was dark enough that Maggie couldn't quite make out whether or not his reaction was disapproving or encouraging. "Yes, I know I shouldn't get too attached but I can't help it."

Court touched her shoulder briefly. "I don't think you can help it. It's part of who you are."

A warm trickle of pleasure ran down her spine. She missed his touch.

Maggie showed him the structure in the center of the village where they would be working the next day. There were no chairs or tables, just a few benches off to the side.

"This is why we brought so much equipment, including tables," she commented as they walked beneath the open-pole shelter. "The chief holds his council meetings here, also ceremonial events. He allows us to use it because he values the medical care we provide. Otherwise it would be off-limits to us foreigners."

"How many patients should we expect?"

"The number varies but it's always a full day.

People will be standing in line by daybreak." Maggie said, heading back the way they had come. "We shouldn't keep the chief waiting."

Court took the flashlight from Maggie and directed the beam out in front of them as they walked back to their hut. Out of necessity, they had to remain close. He could almost fill the hum of happiness radiating off her.

"I take it you and the chief had a good meeting." She'd told him on the way over to the chief's hut that she planned to ask the chief about adopting Neetie.

"Oh, yeah. At first I thought he wouldn't agree. He's concerned about Neetie losing his heritage."

"I assume that you told him differently."

"I reassured him I would honor who he is and his people, and that I only wanted to give him a place to live, food and clothing and most of all love. I had to do a good deal of convincing but he agreed living with me was best for Neetie. He knows the village can't give Neetie what he needs. I promised we would visit often and Neetie could stay for a long visit during school breaks."

"I know you'll give him a wonderful home."

"Now all I have to do is make it legal with the government. I'll start working on that as soon as we get back. So, how did you find dinner with the chief?"

"Interesting. It wasn't my usual fare but it turned out better than I expected." His words carried in the silence of the evening.

"You did better than I expected. You didn't even flinch when you were offered the bowels."

"Thank you, ma'am. I think that might be one of the nicest compliments I've ever received. I'm generally not opposed to new challenges."

"You're certainly braver than most of the visiting doctors we get. I've gotten so used to eating like the locals I don't know that I'd even want to have a steak if offered one."

"I know a wonderful little hole in the wall near Fennel Hall, where they grill the most fantastic steaks," he said. "You visit the next time you're in the States and I'll take you. I think you'll be more than tempted."

"I don't get home often. When I do, I don't travel much."

"It's just an invitation between friends, Maggie, not a binding trade agreement between two countries."

She snorted. "Am I that uptight?"

"Maybe. But you've had a long day. With some rest you should be the same efficient and in-control person you've always been."

"I don't mind the *efficient* description but I'm not sure *in control* is a compliment."

"It is. There's nothing wrong with a woman being strong. I kind of like a woman who knows what she wants."

When they reached the hut she stopped and turned, "Would you mind giving me a few minutes before you come in?"

"Sure. I'll, uh, double-check that the truck is secure."

"Thanks. I'll hurry." Maggie turned and ducked through the doorway.

Court looked up at the star-studded sky and moaned. Maybe he should be gentleman enough to bed down in the truck. Only he'd get more sleep in the hut with Maggie than he would cramped up in the truck with his feet sticking out the window. After killing as much time as possible, Court returned to the hut. He waited a few minutes outside before Maggie pulled the blanket back. "I'm done."

She slipped back inside before Court could grab

the blanket. Entering, he paused, letting his eyes adjust to the dim light provided by the low fire. Maggie had already crawled inside her sleeping bag. The other rolled-up bag lay on his mat across the room.

"There's water in the buckets by the fire if you need to wash up. The one closest is still warm. I left a cloth," she said, before turning her back to him.

Sharing the hut with him didn't seem to be rattling the self-assured Maggie at all. For some reason that disturbed him.

Maggie tried to ignore the rustle of a shirt being removed. Every muscle in her body tightened. Her lungs ached from holding her breath. Would the sound of a zipper be next?

Curiosity had always been her downfall. She couldn't resist the urge to look. Trying to roll as if asleep, she shifted to her back. Her eyes flicked open.

Mercy. She should've never looked.

Court stood with his back to her, bare to the waist. His broad shoulders looked even wider with the flicker of firelight reflecting off the dampness of his back. His pants rode low on his hips. In his bare feet, he took the stance of a Greek god she'd seen on her visit to Greece during high school. The statue had made enough of an impression to be remembered just as Court made one now.

He raised an arm and moved the cloth with easy grace down his arm, causing the muscles in his back to ripple. He repeated the process on his other arm.

Maggie's chest tightened. Had she been in Africa so long she'd become a voyeur? She swallowed the golf-ball-size lump in her throat. She'd never thought she'd enjoy being a peeping Tom but this show was well worth it. Court was an outstanding example of virile male. If she could just touch…

His back remained to her as he said, "You know, the best form of flattery is having someone stare at you." His words rumbled low and rough.

Maggie closed her eyes, went still.

His sexy chuckle rippled through her until she found sleep.

"Missy Maggie, I not feel good."

Court was already getting to his feet as Neetie

finished the last word. Maggie crawled out of her bedroll and asked, "Neetie, what's wrong?"

"Stomach hurt."

Maggie spoke to the woman who had brought Neetie to the hut. She nodded and left. "Well, that shouldn't be too hard to fix. Why don't you let Mister Doctor take a look at you?"

Court didn't move. When would he get past the reluctance he felt each time he had to examine a child? It was his job. Had been his life's calling. But now he didn't seem able to give his patients all he should, especially the children. Sometimes all they required was special attention, and he didn't seem capable even of that any more.

Neetie glanced at him then looked at Maggie. "No, you," the boy said.

The boy's rejection cut deep. Had Court become so unapproachable to children? At one time, his ability to get children to cooperate had been legendary.

He could identify with this child on one level. Court, too, knew what it meant to say goodbye to people you loved forever. That much he and the boy had in common.

It's time to act like the doctor you used to be.

Court went down on one knee, which put him almost at eye level with Neetie. "I promise to do my best to make you feel better if you will tell me where it hurts. Will you trust me?" The words came out haltingly at first but he finally managed the right tone.

Neetie looked at Maggie. She nodded and he looked back at Court. "Okay." Little enthusiasm infused the word but Court would take it.

Maggie knelt beside Court, placing his bag between them. Pulling his stethoscope out of his bag, Court took a fortifying breath. "Can you point to where it hurts?"

"Don't know, it just hurts."

"Let me give you a listen and see if there is more going on. I'll be easy." Court said, placing the disk of the stethoscope on Neetie's thin chest.

"Take a deep breath."

The boy did as instructed, but groaned when he exhaled.

Court had him lie down on Maggie's bedroll. When Court examined Neetie's abdomen he questioned the tightness and the ridge of the liver that was more prominent than it should have been.

"Mister Doctor make me feel better?"

Court gave Neetie an earnest look. "I hope so, Neetie, I hope so."

Never more in his life had he hoped he was telling the truth. Could he live with himself if he was wrong again? "Why don't you stay here tonight? That way Missy Maggie and I can keep an eye on you."

Neetie pushed away, fear on his face. "You going to put an eye on me?"

Court's laughter exploded from deep within him, creating a rumble throughout the hut. Maggie joined him, her mirth soft and sweetly entwined with his. It felt great to laugh. Something that he hadn't done in months, maybe even years.

Controling his merriment, Court rubbed Neetie's head. "No, my man, I will not be putting an eye on you. I'll just check on you."

Maggie settled Neetie into her bedroll. The boy whimpered and rolled into a ball. With the gentle stroking of her hand on his back he calmed and slept.

Court stuffed his stethoscope back into his med bag and placed it beside his bedroll. It had felt good to interact with a child again. He chuckled. If nothing else, they were refreshingly literal.

Hopefully this was nothing more than a simple gastrointestinal event.

He watched as Maggie ran a hand along the boy's cheek and made a soft cooing sound. She loved Neetie. Court's insecurity wouldn't let him trouble her over something he wasn't confident was truly a problem. With any luck Neetie's trouble was nothing more than a simple stomachache.

Court couldn't remember ever seeing a patient's mother treat a child with as much concern as Maggie gave this boy. She'd shown Neetie, who was no real relation, more love and comfort than his mother had ever shown him. For one brief moment, he wished he was on the receiving end of her attention.

His parents had seemed to have only had time for Lyland. He had needed more, understandably, but Court had always felt like an outsider, looking in. Even though he'd been young, he remembered how devastated his parents had been when Lyland had died. Court had been too. He had been his twin brother. The other half of him.

With Lyland gone, his mother and father had concentrated all their time and energy on the work of the foundation. With his older sisters seeing about themselves, he had been left in the care of a nanny, then sent off to boarding school. What few meals their family had shared had revolved around the importance of the work the foundation supported.

A warm strange feeling filled him as he watched Maggie with Neetie. Would that ever be possible in his life? No, he wouldn't let it be. It would hurt too much when it was taken away.

"I saw your face when you were palpating his belly. What's wrong with Neetie?" Maggie's quiet question laden with distress brought him out of his musings.

He hadn't meant to be so transparent. Court moved to sit beside her. "I can't be sure at this stage, but his liver is slightly distended."

"Hepatitis." Maggie said the word like pronouncing a death warrant.

She'd been working in Ghana long enough to recognize the common disease among the people. Court ran a reassuring hand across her shoulders. "I can't say for sure based on what I know so far. It may be a bug. We'll have to wait and see how he does. I'll stay up with him awhile. Why don't you get some sleep?"

Maggie's body seemed to lose some of its rigidness.

"I'm going to sit here awhile. You go ahead. I want to keep the fire going enough to keep him warm."

"Look, Maggie, you can't stay up all night and work all day. I sure can't, especially if I don't have to. Neetie's fine. We're both right here. So what's the real problem?"

She craned her neck back to look up at him, her eyes flashing. "There's only your bedroll left, that's the problem."

"I don't mind sharing."

She screwed up her face at him.

"Don't get your hackles up. We both need some rest. Why don't we spread my bedroll out on the other side of Neetie? That'll put him between us and the fire. You can reach out and check on him during the night."

Maggie opened her mouth to protest but he held up a hand. "Let me finish. We don't have to get in it. There's an extra blanket in my pack we can use for a cover. Will that work?"

She nodded but showed no enthusiasm for his plan as she focused on Neetie. While he arranged their bed Maggie put a couple of small pieces of wood on the fire. By the time he found the blanket, she'd crawled on top of the sleeping bag and lay on her side, with her back to him.

Court stretched out beside her, flipping the all-purpose covering up and over them. She remained as rigid as an iron bar as he settled down. A few quiet minutes passed before he gave in to temptation to lighten the mood and whispered softly, "Remind me to thank Neetie for giving me the opportunity to sleep with you."

Receiving the reward of a quick kick to the shin, he let out a theatrical moan.

CHAPTER FIVE

MAGGIE'S eyes opened as coolness tickled her back. Movement caught her attention, and she watched Court bend down to pick up two pieces of firewood from the small pile near the door. It amazed her that this Boston socialite didn't at all seem out of place in the simple hut.

She laid a hand on Neetie's shoulder. The boy slept comfortably. She breathed a sigh of relief. Maybe Court's concerns had been over top. Surely it was only something Neetie had eaten. She loved him and with the chief's agreement she was so close to becoming the family she'd always dreamed of having.

Court lifted the blanket and crawled underneath, causing her to shiver. "What time is it?"

"Still early. Go back to sleep." His raspy words were warm against her cheek.

She shifted closer to Neetie, putting her arm around the boy and pulling him close. Even so,

Court's warmth touched hers from head to toe. He put a long arm across her and Neetie, sandwiching her between them.

"I don't—"

"Shut up, Maggie, and go back to sleep."

A sliver of light ran under the thick material covering the doorway when Maggie next woke. Still in the shadowy part of slumber, Maggie found her head cushioned by a muscular arm. A cocoon of warmth surrounded her. She wiggled, snuggling back against the feeling.

"Mmm, that's nice." Court's gruff voice came from behind her.

Maggie eyes jerked open.

She lay spoon fashion against Court and his hand rested beneath her right breast. She wrapped her hand around his wrist and pushed it away. Along with his hand went the splendid warmth and pleasure of being touched. She'd been alone so long she forgot how good it felt to have a man embrace her.

"I'm hungry," Neetie said.

She heard Court's low expletive as he moved away.

Maggie ran her hand over Neetie's forehead. "So you're feeling better?"

The boy nodded.

"Come on, Neetie, let's give Maggie some privacy and find you something to eat." Standing, Court looked down on them like a god hovering above.

Maggie watched as the two males left, the tall, strong man giving his entire attention to the painfully thin boy, a solid muscular arm about slender shoulders. The action was the first familiar one Court had made toward Neetie. Until the night before he'd kept the boy at arm's length, never completely giving Neetie his full attention. It was as if something that had been closed off in Court had been set free as he'd taken care of Neetie.

The morning had been busy. Court had never doubted it would be. Waking with Maggie in his arms, warm and soft against him, had made the morning seem even longer. He only had to let his mind slip away from the next patient for an instant to want to feel her in his arms again. But just because he wanted her sexually, it didn't mean he cared for her, he reminded himself.

He'd been attracted to women before but watching the subtle sway of her hips in the thin floral skirt as she walked around the makeshift clinic was enough to make him dream of things that could never be. How in the world was he going to survive sharing a hut with her again tonight? Even with Neetie there it would be more than he could stand.

Court glanced to where she was examining one of the children. She smiled at the mother, telling her what a fine baby boy she had, before she picked up the chubby child and blew on his belly. When the baby giggled so did she. The sound captivated Court, having never heard anything like it. He wished he could be the one giving her so much pleasure. Maggie was creeping into a spot where he'd never let another human enter.

A woman wearing a colorful turban approached Maggie and spoke rapidly to her. All the joy drained from Maggie's face. She handed the baby back to the mother. Maggie's stricken look made him thankful there weren't any more patients waiting.

He went to her, placing his hands on her shoulders. "What's wrong, Maggie? What has happened?"

She looked up at him, her eyes shinny with moisture. "Neetie collapsed."

"Where is he?"

"In Zena's hut."

"I'll get my bag. Then you show me where."

As he and Maggie wove their way through the village, Court mentally kicked himself. He'd had a nagging feeling all morning that Neetie's problem wasn't going to be simple. Still, they couldn't have dashed off in the middle of the night into the middle of nowhere. It wouldn't have been just Neetie in trouble. He had Maggie to think of too. If he'd been at home he would've ordered an abdominal ECHO but the closest ECHO was to hell and gone from this remote village.

Neetie lay on a mat in the hut, eyes wide with fear. Maggie ran the last few feet to him. Bending down, she took his hand. "Oh, honey, are you all right? What happened?" She put the back of her hand on his forehead, checking for a fever.

Court moved to the other side of Neetie. "Maggie, make sure he remains still while I examine him."

Maggie blinked and assumed her nursing demeanor. She moved so Neetie could see her. "Stay still so Dr. Court can listen to you."

Court put his stethoscope to the boy's chest and listened. Then, using his fingertips, he moved them slowly along the boy's tight abdomen until he found the upper edge of his liver. It was enlarged, worse than it had been the night before. This time he had no doubt.

"What's wrong?" Maggie demanded.

He didn't want to say the words out loud, hated having to give parents bad news about their child. Court wished someone else was there to tell Maggie what was wrong with Neetie. He looked into Maggie's big, green-eyed expectant gaze. "It's hepatitis. B or C. I can't be sure which until I run some tests."

At her stricken look, he ached to take her in his arms and tell her it would be all right, but he couldn't make such a promise.

"Neetie, you need to take it easy for the rest of the day." Court worked to keep his voice even, reassuring. "Do you have a friend who can play a quiet game with you?"

Neetie shifted and sat up on his own, nodding agreement.

"Maggie and I need to finish our work but we'll be back to check on you, okay?" Court stood. He rubbed the top of the boy's head, before he offered Maggie his hand. She took it and he helped her to stand. She removed her fingers from his as soon as she could.

They were in the bright sunlight a moment before she turned to him and pinned him with a look. "Shouldn't we leave for the hospital?"

"You know better than I that we can't travel across this land at night. I'm sure you also know that all we can do for Neetie right now is let him rest and make sure he eats good-quality food and drinks often. He'll recover with care and time. Why don't you let me do the worrying?"

"I'm a big girl. I can handle worry." She stepped closer, biting out the words, "You don't decide what I worry about or don't worry about. You're only here for a little while and I'll still be here when you're gone."

She turned so fast her ponytail and hips swung as she stalked off.

Maggie spoke out of her fear for Neetie but her

words still stung. Court followed her as she set a brisk pace back toward the clinic area. Her work at the accident and the pragmatic way she'd accepted his verdict about Raja's leg told him she was used to unpleasant news. Still, Neetie wasn't just anyone to her. She reacted out of love where Neetie was concerned. It wasn't about his insecurities, but about her. He had to keep telling himself that.

Maggie had too difficult a life already. A young pretty woman like her shouldn't be spending her time in such a stark, unforgiving place. Those rhinestones on her flip-flops hinted at the fact she might enjoy parties, plays and fine dining. Something about Maggie made him want to make her life easier, to give her those things—make her smile. She had a beautiful smile but it didn't often push the concerns of life from her eyes.

By the time he'd returned to the clinic, Maggie had already organized the waiting villagers into two groups, those she would tend and those who would require his attention.

"You'll need to see the doctor," she said in Mamprusi to a bone-thin old man, her tone sweet with concern. Maggie led the elderly man to Court and in short, concise words told him what was wrong. So went the rest of the afternoon and into the early evening.

While he was debriding the wound on his last patient, Maggie asked him, "Do you need help? If not, I want to check on Neetie."

"I'm good here." He waited until her looked met his. "We did good work today."

He received a curt nod before she began packing with her usual efficiency. He hoped his olive-branch statement cleared the air between them.

Maggie pulled the strap of the large med pack over her shoulder and turned to leave. She hadn't missed Court's attempt to set things right between them. It'd been years since she'd allowed something someone said to upset her so. Court managed to change that.

The last time had been when Ted had told her their wedding was off. Hurt had morphed into resentment and was soon on the road to becoming destructive ire. She'd promised herself then she'd never allow another person to have such power over her emotions again. She'd rebounded with difficulty, had made a life in Ghana, had accepted who she was and looked forward to being Neetie's mother. Them being a family.

She'd found happiness and peace until Court had shown up in his glistening plane with his good looks and easy charm. The guy had gotten to her enough to make her fighting mad, bringing back all those destructive feelings. She wouldn't let Court take away the contentment she'd work so hard to achieve. Maggie refused to let him matter. All her energy should be directed toward getting Neetie healthy again. She didn't need Court carrying her burdens.

Could her resentment be a defense against her growing attraction to Court? He was like a tall, cool drink of water that would soon evaporate, leaving an unquenchable thirst behind. Picking up her pace to power-walk speed, she made her way through the village.

Maggie found Neetie sitting cross-legged on the floor, playing a stick game with a friend.

"Hey, Neetie. How're you feeling?" He shrugged her hand away when she placed it on his forehead. From appearances, Neetie looked as if he wasn't ill at all. Maybe Court had been right, and she'd overreacted. She'd never seen him offer anything but his best to the patients he'd care for.

"Good. I hungry."

"Well, that's a great sign." She stood. "Let's get you something to eat."

"I want to stay here." He looked at Zena with questioning eyes. She agreed and Maggie could hardly insist Neetie come with her. He wasn't hers yet and this was his opportunity to be with his friends, even if she needed a buffer between her and Court.

"Okay, but you have to promise to eat and drink for Zena."

"I will."

It had become dark by the time Court left Neetie. The boy felt better and for that Court was grateful. He hadn't noticed Maggie slipping out as he'd examined Neetie. Court left Neetie playing happily with a friend, and drove the Jeep around the outskirts of the village, parking it beside his and Maggie's hut. When he entered their shelter he fully expected Maggie to be in her bedroll but she wasn't.

A woman's resentment had never registered

with him before but disappointing Maggie made his insides draw up in knots. He wanted to make it right between them, to find that relaxed spot he hadn't known existed until it was gone. A place where he felt good about himself, something he'd not experienced in a long time. Not since the night he'd left his practice.

Picking up a bedroll, he resisted the urge to share a sleeping bag with Maggie again. He snapped out their sleeping bags, taking special care to place hers on one side of the fire and his on the other. He washed up, using the pail of water and sliver of soap Maggie had left for him. She still didn't come into the hut.

Where was she?

Maggie moved around the village and surrounding area comfortably, but he couldn't forget her warning about wild animals and being out alone. Pulling a clean T-shirt over his head and tugging it into place, he impatiently shoved the blanket door back as a flash of lightning cut across the sky. He headed out into the night.

During a second flash he saw Maggie standing well away from the huts. What was she doing? At a brisk pace he walked toward her, slowing as he came to stand beside her. Another flash showed her silhouetted against the blue-black of the horizon. She stood with her arms wrapped around her waist, her head back as she looked into the sky. He stopped a few paces from her.

"I'm sorry. It's just I love the kid so much."

Court stepped closer. "I know. I can see that. Anyone can see that, Maggie."

"Just the thought that I could lose him…it's just too much."

"I know."

"No, you don't. You don't know what it's like to be this scared."

He kicked at the ground with his boot. When he didn't respond, she turned to face him. Even though he couldn't see her clearly, he sensed her intent look.

"Do you?" The word came out as a plea to know.

Why couldn't she let it go? If she would, he wouldn't have to go to that dark, insecure place. But if he did talk about it, left those ugly feelings here in this vast country with Maggie, maybe he could find reconciliation. "I was scared about making the right diagnosis." Each word he had to force from his mouth. *Because I couldn't risk making the same mistake I'd made before.*

"But I've seen you make diagnoses in the clinic all day without flinching and now you hesitate? I want to know why." The tone of her voice was aggressive, demanding an answer.

He shoved his hands into his pockets and turned away from her, looking out into the vast night, hoping it would swallow him. His chest constricted to even think about the past. Another boy's life, the child of Court's boyhood friend. The loss of his brother and the gaping hole it had left. Maggie cared about Neetie. What would happen to her if Neetie was ever as ill as Lyland had been? How Jimmy had been when Court had made the wrong decision?

The gentle touch of Maggie's hand on his forearm brought him out of the black memories.

"The type of patients we were seeing today was straightforward. A boil needs to be lanced and bandaged. A cut needs to be cleaned and covered. Bones break and need to be set. No guesswork there. With Neetie it is more difficult to know. To judge the seriousness."

She shifted to stand in front of him. "But you

were right about Neetie. What happened to make you distrust yourself?"

Did she read minds? How transparent was he? Did she feel the pain of a mistake and recognize it in him?

"Court?"

She moved closer. He felt the brush of her against him. She stood in his personal space both physically and emotionally. The desire to step away flooded him but the slight squeeze of her fingers encouraged him to stay put. What would she think of him if he explained? He knew her well enough now to know she wouldn't let it go. "One of my patients, Jimmy, the son of my school friends growing up, wasn't feeling well. I saw him in my office that afternoon." His words sounded hollow, distant, as if he spoke about someone else. "That night the Armstrong Foundation held its annual fundraising gala. My parents had given me the job of schmoozing a possible major medical benefactor. In the middle of the discussion I received a page telling me Jimmy was in the ER. I didn't go. Jimmy had had a reaction to the medicine I'd prescribed. He now has brain damage, all because of some insane need of mine to impress my parents." Each word of the last sentence was like acid dropped from between clenched teeth. He felt as if a boulder lay on his chest and he was struggling to push it off so he could breathe.

In the dark, he couldn't see if Maggie was judging him, didn't want to see. He'd already judged himself, and pronounced himself guilty.

"You couldn't have known."

He let out a huff of self-disgust. His muscles became taut with tension. "I couldn't be bothered to even go in to see my own patient." The words came out whip-sharp. "For heaven's sake, I'm a doctor and Jimmy is the son of my best friend. Getting big bucks for the foundation and meeting my father's demands wasn't worth that boy's life or his family's." She flinched but didn't move away from him.

"You know that isn't true."

"Maybe not, but that's how I felt, feel."

He lashed out at himself, not her. When she said nothing he continued, "There was an investigation. I wasn't found to be negligent but I don't believe it."

The reassuring flex of her fingers encouraged him. "Even though I don't always agree with the foundation's decisions, I do know its work helps people." Her voice took on a strong tone. "You're a good doctor. I've watched you work and interact with the villagers, the people at the hospital clinic. Except with… What happened with the boy is why you won't see the children unless you are forced to, isn't it?"

"I'm a children's doctor, afraid of children," he said in complete disgust.

"No, you're not. I admit that I didn't understand it. Didn't really like you because of it. But you were great with Neetie last night and I have no complaints about your interaction with the child today. You are good with them."

"Jimmy's about the same age as Neetie. I had to make myself remember how to interact with a child. Neetie's such an open kid he let me in, trusted me. When the door opened I became determined never to let it close again. I had a few moments today that were rough but I made it."

"I think you did an outstanding job. You're an excellent doctor, the best I've seen, actually."

He grasped her hand on his arm, as if she were his lifeline to sanity and interlocked her fingers with his. "I appreciate your confidence. I took a leave of absence. I needed time to think. When your letter came across my desk I thought it would give me an opportunity to review the hospital's work and to stick my toe back into working with patients. I had no idea of how far I would wade in."

"I bet."

"When Neetie got sick, I was afraid it was all happening again. I like Neetie. I don't want to fail him like I did Jimmy."

He couldn't believe he had admitted to such fear. A doctor was supposed to be confident in his decisions, and if he wasn't, he needed to at least act as if he was. But he couldn't, no, wouldn't, mess up again.

"Have you spoken to the boy's family? They may be more understanding than you are being with yourself."

No. He couldn't face Roger. He couldn't make the boy better. "I don't think they want to see me."

"You might be surprised." Her voice sounded warm with compassion.

A big fat drop of rain landed on his forehead. Another splattered on his arm.

"The rainy season has begun," Maggie an-

nounced with awe. "A time for a new beginning."
She lightly squeezed his hand.

Was there a double meaning there? Tough
Maggie, who fixed everything for everybody,
seemed to be fixing him also. It felt wonderful
to be traveling back to where he belonged.

She tugged on his hand, then let it go. "Come on.
We'd better run if we don't want to get soaked."

Maggie searched her bag a few minutes later to
find a clean, dry shirt. Across the hut Court did the
same. She glanced at him and found him watching her with an intent look. His eyes dropped to
where her wet shirt molded to her breast. Her nipples hardened, pushing against her thin sports bra.
She pulled on the material in an effort to make
her reaction less visible.

His mood had changed from one of deep remorse to ease as they'd run to get out of the rain.
His full-bodied laugh had filled the hut as they'd
both tried to get thought the narrow opening at
the same time. She hadn't been able to help but
join him in his mirth.

But now the air between them reminded her of
the lightning they had been watching earlier, hot
with expectancy. Maggie took a deep breath, and

tried to add some firmness to her tone when she said, "Be a gentleman."

"Do I have to?" A wolfish, predatory smile curved his lips. "There should be some perks to having to stay in a simple hut in the middle of nowhere."

She gave him her best piercing look but her fortitude weakened as his unwavering stare made her breasts tingle. A stream of heat curled within her but she held the unwavering stance.

With an exaggerated sigh he turned his back. "You sure know how to disappoint a guy."

"I'm confident there are plenty of women in Boston you could ogle."

The rasp of his zipper caught her attention. She didn't dare look over her shoulder but she was tempted. *Concentrate on what you are doing. Get into those dry clothes pronto.*

"I imagine there are a few."

She heard the humor and the self-assurance in his voice.

His lack of doctor-patient confidence hadn't affected his male ego.

Maggie jerked on a dry undershirt, wishing with all her heart she had another dry bra. The thin material of her shirt didn't seem like enough protection from Court's fire-starter stare.

She arranged her short knit shorts so she could get into them quickly. She wasn't normally such a prude. Was it that she didn't trust Court or didn't trust herself? The feelings he evoked had lain dormant for so long she couldn't trust herself. She slipped out of her wet panties, pulled off the flimsy, damp skirt and jerked on her shorts. "Jealous?"

"Jealous?"

She spun around. "Why would I be jealous?"

Court pulled his olive-colored cargo shorts up over his hips. She watched in fascination as notch by notch he pulled his zipper into place, leaving the button of his pants open.

"Come on, Maggie, you've been in the wilds too long. I'm kidding you. I'm not a monk but I'm no Casanova either."

She removed the band holding her hair and swung it back and forth in an effort to fan it out so it would dry quicker. It would look a mess in the morning if she didn't comb it.

A hissing sound came from his direction. She turned. A tingle ran up her spine, and the small room closed in on her, making the sleeping arrangements even more intimate. "What?"

"I've never seen your hair down. It's beautiful."

Her cheeks heated. "You've been in the wilds too long. It's a mess and will be worse in the morning." She searched her bag for she couldn't remember what.

Their shared laugher and smothering heat of the past few minutes were the first she'd shared with a man in a long time. It felt nice to be desired. Especially by a man as intriguing as Court, to want him to touch her, kiss her, make love to her...

Relief washed over her when she turned and found Court putting a log on the fire and crawling into his sleeping bag. He turned his back to the fire and her. Court had been giving her a hard time just to make her feel uncomfortable. To get them both back on an even keel.

Thunder rolled in the distance as Maggie slipped into her sleeping bag. She punched at the extra blanket doubling as a pillow. There was more thunder but closer this time. Maggie flipped over on her side. At another blast of thunder she rolled again. She couldn't decide whether she couldn't sleep because of the weather or the fact that Court lay nearby.

Somehow his declaration earlier had built a bridge between them. Even though she was an easy person to talk to, he would also leave those admissions behind when he left. She wouldn't be a content reminder of his weakness. That brokenness in him made him even more likeable.

A flash of light filled the narrow opening around the edges of the door covering as it ruffled in the breeze. Seconds later a boom filled the air and shook the earth beneath her. She sat ramrod straight, letting out a squeak.

"Maggie?"

"I'm fine. It caught me by surprise." She lay back again and curled into a ball, shutting her eyes tightly. Could she disappear into the ground?

"Maggie, you're shaking." The temperature had dropped but Court would bet that wasn't causing her chills. Fearless Maggie was fighting some demon.

With a whoosh of the zipper he undid her sleeping bag and laid it flat on the ground.

"What're you doing?"

He couldn't help but enjoy her indignation.

"You're shivering. I already have one sick person to worry over and I'm not taking any chances with you. The temperature dropped and you need warmth. I can provide that." Even if it killed him doing it. "Scoot over." He stretched out beside her and pulled his sleeping bag over them. She accepted the situation, seeming to have lost all energy to fight.

"I'm not cold," she murmured, looking toward the fire, her back to him.

"Then you're afraid of storms?"

"No, I'm not afraid of storms. I'm afraid of memories," she muttered.

Court didn't say anything. This lovely woman who lived in the glaring reality of death every day might have more in common with him than he'd thought. Was she also running from an ugly past?

His fingers itched to stroke her hair. If he did, could he resist running his hands through it, putting his face it, inhaling the scent of it? He balled his hands into fists, stopping the fantasy, and said, "Want to talk about it?"

The concept of caring enough to listen was alien to him. Keeping an emotional distance had always been his trademark. Love or care too much and you got hurt.

"Maggie, you can talk to me." He made his tone a soft, reassuring one, as if to one of his young patients. He shifted on to his side and propped his head in his hand. At least one hand stayed under control.

She kept her back to him but after a deep breath she started to speak, less to him and more to some unknown spot on the other side of the hut.

"It was raining that night." The words came out haltingly, as if they had been bottled up and now the top was being removed. Each word fizzed out under pressure. "I was late getting off work. A last-minute emergency. I still had to change. My girlfriends were giving me a lingerie party." She rolled onto her back, and instead of facing him she looked at where the thatch of the roof met at a point above. She studied it as if she watched a motion-picture screen.

Court didn't move. He didn't want to risk interrupting her, stop her from talking.

"I was so excited. I was going to be married in two weeks. I thought Ted was the love of my life."

Irrational as it was, he felt a pang of an unknown emotion to know she'd cared so deeply for another man.

With a shaky breath she said, "We planned to have lots of children."

Court watched one large tear slipped down her cheek. Still, he didn't touch her. Her tone said she would appreciate it. She wanted no one to feel sorry for her.

"What happened? Tell me." He pushed a lock of hair away from her face. "I've shared my ugly secret."

Maggie went still as if she was processing the truth of that statement. She whispered, "The car skidded, and rolled and rolled. I was trapped, crushed. The doctors said I'd live but I'd never have children."

"I'm sorry." Since he'd met her he'd seen daily demonstrations of how much she loved children. For any woman it would be devastating but for Maggie it must have seemed like a death sentence.

"That wasn't the worst."

He strained to hear her.

"I would've adopted but my fiancé didn't see it that way. Although he did have the decency to wait until I was out of the hospital before he told me the wedding was off. In his family, producing a child is a sign of virility in a man. He wouldn't marry someone who couldn't have children."

Court's curse word filled the air.

"I couldn't agree with you more," Maggie said, regaining some of her feistiness. "I'd been stamped imperfect."

"I know about imperfection and that's not true about you. You're a perfect nurse, a perfect mother for Neetie, a perfect friend, perfect listener. There is no way a person with as big a heart as yours could ever be imperfect. Look at me." His words were stern as he waited until her moisture-filled eyes met his gaze. "I don't want you to ever say that about yourself again."

Unable to stand it any longer, he enveloped her in his arms.

Maggie placed a soft kiss on the warm skin beneath his lips. It tasted salty but there was another spice there that was all Court. Unable to resist, she pressed her lips against him again, and savored his taste. He was so warm, comforting, caring.

A sharp hiss came from above her head and she felt Court's body tense. "Maggie, I don't think…"

He knew pain. Knew what it was to fail someone. She kissed his chest again, before looking up.

"Maggie, I don't want you to regret this in the morning."

Still his mouth didn't come closer. Her hand slid to his waist and she kneaded his skin with the tips of her fingers. Time seemed to become an eternity before his mouth found hers. It had been worth the wait. His lips were cool and dry. A white-hot stream of need shot though her. Court allowed her freedom to explore, but made no effort to deepen or control the kiss. Maggie feasted as Court remained uninvolved.

When she groaned in complaint, he pulled back. "Whether or not we act on this up to you but know that if we do, there'll be no holding back. Also know I'm not your future. It would only be two people enjoying each other."

"I'm a big girl. I know what I'm doing."

Like iron to a magnet, her hand wrapped around the nape of his neck. Fingers combing through his hair, she tugged him closer. Her back arched in her eagerness to have him near. Her hand slid up from his waist to rest on his warm, hard chest. Smoothing her fingertips across the fine hair,

Maggie reveled in the feel of him. His muscles rippled beneath his skin in response to her touch. Mewling in frustration, she touched the tip of her tongue to the crease of his lips, begging him to join her.

He accepted the invitation.

Court opened for her, his tongue twisting and teasing hers as she drew him closer. The moment was perfect. She been in the dry wilds too long and Court was a welcome storm.

Dared she ask for or want more?

As if his control had snapped, he stretched out further and pinned her legs with one of his, gathering her to him. Maggie burrowed against him, unable to get close enough. He became master of their kiss, made demands she welcomed. Maggie had no complaints; she wanted it all. Offered it all.

Court leaned back and yanked the sleeping bag away. His hand ran across her belly, gathering a handful of thin T-shirt as he brought her closer. Her knee slipped between his thighs. Releasing the shirt material, his long fingers traveled up to cover a breast. He lifted and weighed it, before flicking a finger across the puckered tip.

Removing his lips from hers, he said, "Perfect,"

before he brushed small kisses along her cheek as his head moved downward. Her fingers caressed his dark strands of hair as his mouth drew her nipple, shirt and all, into the warm cavern of his mouth. A sizzle of pleasure filled her.

His head lifted, a small chuckle of male satisfaction tumbling from him. "Liked that, did you?"

At Maggie's slight nod, his sexy grin grew larger and his eyes blazed. "Then we both should enjoy this even more."

His hand pushed at her shirt until he'd bared her breasts. With the same show of control she'd found so excessively aggravating earlier, he lowered his lips to reclaim their prize. This time hot, begging skin was blanketed in sweet, soothing moisture.

Court gave his complete attention to first one breast and then the other. His hand moved lower on her flat stomach. He paused when his fingers touched the long scar that lay off to the right side.

His eyes lifted in question.

She winced as the memories flooded back. "The car accident."

He moved his hands so they rested at the curve of her waist. "I'm sorry." He kissed the spot and the memories were securely locked away again. A feeling of being cared for and understood filled her. Only a few had seen the nasty scar but none had reacted as Court had.

"Thank you." She tugged him up. Wrapping her arms around his waist, she kissed him in gratitude.

Court shifted so he lay on top of her. Maggie loved the pressure of his weight and the bliss that the fluttering kisses along her neck and behind her ear were producing. She shivered.

The hand on her breast stilled. Maggie's looked flashed in the direction of where the sound had come. Zena stood in the doorway.

"Neetie sick."

CHAPTER SIX

COURT'S gut clenched. That elated mood he'd felt while making love to Maggie was instantly replaced with the old festering feeling of self-doubt and loathing he'd carried for so long. Once again he'd been too distracted to check up on his little patient.

Maggie was already heading out the hut door by the time he grabbed his medical bag and followed. They climbed into the truck and drove around to where Neetie was staying. Maggie jumped out before he'd parked the truck.

He found Neetie lying in the fetal position on a pallet to one side of the hut. Maggie was on her knees beside him, and she looked at him, her eyes full of expectancy. Court's chest constricted further. She trusted him to make it better. He sure hoped he deserved her belief in him. He'd disappointed others before but he planned never to let it happen again.

"His fever has spiked." Panic filled her voice as it rose an octave. "I'll get some water and start trying to bring the fever down."

Maggie sprang to her feet, dashing across the floor. Court breathed a sigh of relief. If she was in nursing mode, she would worry less. "Now, Neetie, tell me where it hurts."

Neetie stretched out his legs and rubbed his side.

Court felt Neetie's lower right quadrant with the tips of his fingers. It was tender and the ridge of his liver more prominent than it had been earlier.

Neetie rubbed high on his arm. "My shoulder hurts too."

"I'll give you something to help you feel better in a minute. I need to check you out first." Court reached into his bag and took out his stethoscope.

He was listening to Neetie's heart when Maggie returned. She dropped to her knees again and dipped a cloth into a bucket before placing it on Neetie's forehead.

He took out a small penlight and said, "Neetie, look at me a minute."

Neetie rolled his head toward Court.

He shined the light into Neetie's eyes.

The sharp intake of Maggie's breath told him

she'd seen it too. The churning building in Court's stomach became more pronounced. He had to get control of the situation, manage the panic growing in him, in her. He didn't want to scare the boy.

She clasped his arm. "His eyes are yellow."

"The hepatitis has advanced. Rapidly. I'll need to do tests to know how bad it is." He hoped he'd caught it early enough to save the boy's life. This time Court wasn't at some gala but he was just as helpless being so far away from adequate medical care. He was going to do all he could for Neetie, unlike what he'd done for his other patient. At least he was here for his patient this time.

"We're going to need to leave at first light to return to the hospital. I don't want him moved. He'll need to stay here tonight."

"I'm going to sit up with him. I'll tell Zena."

"He needs a fever reducer. Go get some bottled water out of the truck."

When Maggie returned she helped Neetie sit upright to take the medicine and tucked him in again.

"I'm going to pack up and go speak to the chief," Court said.

Maggie didn't even notice when he left she was so absorbed in caring for Neetie.

An hour later Court entered the hut with two sleeping bags under his arm to find Maggie still sitting beside Neetie.

She looked up in surprise. "What're you doing here? You should be getting some sleep."

"He's my patient and I'm going to be here if he needs me." Court dropped the rolls on the floor. "I brought you this so you could lie down. Get some rest."

"I'm not going to sleep. Neetie may call out for me."

"Okay, if neither of us are going to sleep then we might as well be comfortable."

Court opened one of the sleeping bags and spread it out on the floor between Neetie and the wall of the hut. He sat down, leaned his back against the wall and patted the space next to him. With a sigh Maggie got up and came to sit down beside him. During the wee hours of the morning Court felt her head lean against his upper arm. Court put an arm around her shoulders and cradled her head to his chest.

* * *

He woke with a start. Neetie had moaned. Maggie set up also, rubbing her eyes.

"It's almost daylight. I'm going to examine him. You go get a couple of blankets out of the truck to wrap him in and let's get him loaded."

Maggie hurried out the door and returned with the blankets.

"Spread the blankets out and let's wrap him up. He doesn't need to be further chilled by the rain."

He and Maggie worked together with their usual efficiency, each anticipating what the other would do. He'd never been more in sync with another person in his life. He found comfort in that feeling. In record time they had Neetie stretched out in the backseat of the truck.

Court pulled out of the village while Neetie still slept. Maggie couldn't keep from touching him as if checking to see if he was still alive. Her lips were taut with worry. Court wanted to ease the strain but he was just as concerned.

He'd questioned the less-than-desirable road trip to the village but the drive back was turning out to be even worse. The pouring rain made mud out of the inches of dry dirt. If what they had traveled coming in could loosely be called a road, it was now a slippery mud field.

"You're worried, aren't you?" Maggie asked, as if she didn't want to hear his answer. "You promised to tell me the truth."

He glanced at her, took her hand and squeezed, trying to put reassurance he didn't feel into the touch. "I am concerned but Neetie's young and I think we've caught the hepatitis early. What we must concentrate on now is getting him back to the hospital as soon as possible."

"I trust your judgment."

He gave her a dry smile. "Thanks. I don't want anything to happen to Neetie either. You didn't get much sleep last night. Why don't you get some rest now? If Neetie needs you, I'll let you know."

"You didn't get much sleep either."

"I'll let you drive when I get tired. Come on." He put a hand on her shoulder and guided her head down to his thigh. She settled against his leg. A shot of awareness whipped through him. He liked having her near, could get used to it. He had to rest his hand on her waist because he had to shift gear and there was nowhere else to put it. It troubled him to see Maggie so upset about

Neetie. For both their sakes, he hoped they could get Neetie to the care he needed in time.

A moan from behind her woke Maggie. She scrambled to sit up in the seat and turned round.

"Missy Maggie, I not feel good." Neetie's eyes were open but the whites were yellow and the veins dark red with fever. He'd pushed the blanket down to his legs. "Hot."

"I know, honey. Would you like a drink of water?"

He nodded but so slightly and pitifully she wanted to cry. But she wouldn't break down, it would only scare him.

"Hey, buddy," Court called over his shoulder. "We'll get you feeling better soon."

Maggie held the bottle of water for Neetie. He took a few sips. A little dribbled down his chin and she wiped it away.

"It's been long enough that he can have more pain-reliever," Court said.

"You're not concerned about his liver being damaged further?"

"Not at this point. We need to keep the fever in check."

She pulled a thermometer out of the med bag and took Neetie's temperature.

It had gone down but not as far as she would have liked. Finding the medicine, she encouraged him to take it. As he held her wrist to sit up, she noticed his hands had swollen.

A rush of alarm ran through her. Because of the dim light, had she not seen the symptom earlier or it had been a recent development? Either way, Neetie was getting worse.

"Honey, you go back to sleep. We'll be at the hospital soon." With shaking hands she tucked him in again.

She touched Court's arm, gaining his attention. "His hands are starting to swell." She saw him tense, and she pushed down the sob that built in her.

"Is there a quicker way to get back than the one we're taking?"

"Yes, but it's more difficult, especially in this weather."

"We don't have a choice."

She glanced at Neetie. Afraid that she might be sick, she focused on what had to be done. "Stay due south."

* * *

Maggie woke from a drowsy state to the whine of tires spinning. She sat upright.

"What's wrong?"

"We're stuck." Disgust filled Court's voice.

"Stuck how?"

"Crossing a stream."

"The flash floods! I was so worried about Neetie I forgot to say anything about them. We need to get out of this before the water starts rising."

"Another downside to living in this God-forsaken place," he muttered, before shifting the truck into reverse and then back into forward while applying the gas. The truck rocked back and forth but still didn't budge.

Maggie looked back at Neetie. He seemed to be sleeping more comfortably. "Neetie?"

"He's fine. Scoot over here and drive. I'll get out and push," he instructed her.

Court climbed out and swiftly disappeared. Maggie worked her way over the gearshift to get behind the wheel. She looked out the open door. Court was in the process of struggling to get to his feet by supporting himself with the door.

"Are you okay?"

"It's slick out here."

She wanted to smile even as worried as she was about Neetie, being stuck or, worse, washed away but she couldn't help finding Court's predicament funny. Maybe her emotions were getting the better of her but Court's fancy big-city backside being covered in mud struck her as comical. In a low growl he said, "If I even think you're laughing…"

"I'm not, I'm not, I promise." She snorted, almost losing control. Their situation wasn't good but a little laugh did help ease the tension.

"When I slap on the side of the truck you give it some gas and, for God's sake, don't put it in reverse."

Court didn't wait for her reply. She pulled the door closed. At the signal thump she checked one more time to make sure the truck was in first gear and pushed the gas petal slowly to the floor. The truck moved forward but not enough to get out of the mire.

Thump. Thump. She let off the gas. Court stood at the door. There wasn't a dry thread on him and a steady stream of water ran off the brim of his hat. She rolled the window down.

"It's not working," he said, breathless. "I'm going to have to unload the wooden supply box and bust it up. I'll use the wood to hopefully get some traction. Cover Neetie with the other blanket. He doesn't need to be in a draft or get wet."

Again Court didn't wait for her reply. Maggie rolled the window up. She watched in the side mirror as he headed for the back of the truck, holding on for support. He had a plan. If she had to be stuck, she was grateful he was with her.

Getting on her knees in the seat so she could reach over Nettie, she covered him. A gust of wind hit her in the face. Court had opened the tailgate. The heavy tarp fluttered above her. For a brief moment she cupped Neetie's face. Thank goodness his temperature hadn't risen.

Opening the door, she hung on to it, making sure she found her footing before moving to the back of the truck. Court had already found the box he was looking for and was unloading the contents by the time she'd joined him.

"Get back inside." He wasn't pleased to see her.

"No, I'm going to help you."

"I can get this. You go stay dry."

"Too late for your chivalry. And I know where the hammer is stored, and you don't. Help me onto the tailgate. I think I can reach it without unloading everything."

"Turn around and I'll help you up. It figures you'd find some way to be in charge," he said in a flat tone that would've been a teasing one under other circumstances.

Careful not to slip, she turned until her backside was to the end of the truck. Court's hands closed around her waist and he lifted her until she sat on the tailgate. Maggie searched through the built-in toolbox, located the hammer and handed it to him.

"You stay out of the rain while I break this box down."

"I can help." Before he could argue she jumped down, splashing mud all over both of them.

"Thanks, Maggie."

"Sorry," she said contritely, even though they both grinned.

As Court demolished the wood carton she stacked the pieces on the tailgate. When he'd finished Court begin pushing wood under the right back tire. Maggie followed his example under the other rear tire. The water had risen, making it difficult to see what she was doing. She felt along the tire to make sure the wood was in place.

"You get in and do what you did before. Let's see if we can get this monster out this time."

Using caution, Maggie made her way back to

the driver's door and climbed into the vehicle. For the first time in her life she flipped a long wet strand of hair out of her face without securing it. She put the truck in gear. Rolling down the window, she yelled, "Ready?"

At the double slap she gave the truck gas. To begin with nothing happened, only the whine of the tires spinning without purpose and the roar of the motor, then with a jerk the truck lurched forward. She brought it to a stop on firmer ground twenty feet away.

Opening the door, she shouted, "I'll drive for a while." She reached behind the passenger seat and pulled out her duffel bag. Unzipping it, she found a dry T-shirt and a towel. The passenger door opened and Court climbed in holding his right hand in the air. Blood ran in streams down his arm.

"What happened?" Her voice rose in alarm.

"Calm down. I'm fine. It's just a cut. How's Neetie?"

"Sleeping. A sure sign he's sick. He would've been talking up a storm in his excitement about being stuck if he wasn't. Here, wrap this around your hand." She passed him her T-shirt.

Digging through the supply bag, she found a

bottle of water. "Stretch your hand over here and out the window and let me wash it off enough to see how bad it is."

He did, leaning hard against her. "I might get hurt more often if I get to do this."

"Just like a man to take advantage of every opportunity," she quipped without taking her eyes off what she was doing. She poured water over his hand, working toward the injury. She flinched at his hiss of pain when the liquid found his open wound. "I'm sorry."

"Has to be done."

She continued to pour water and use a gauze pad to clean the area. There was something she liked about caring for this big, strong man, just as she like having him care for her. Becoming so self-sufficient, she hadn't realized that particular element had been missing in her life. "How did you do this?"

"I was pushing on the tailgate when the truck finally came out of the hole. My hand raked down the gate. There must've been a piece of metal sticking out."

The two-inch-long gash continued to bleed across the palm of his hand and down his wrist.

"Woh, this looks pretty bad."

"I'll be fine. Put some butterfly strips over it and I'll have it looked at when we get to the hospital. We've got to go."

"I'll do that for now but you'll need a few stitches and an antibiotic."

"Stop fussing, Nurse." He moved back into his seat, still holding her shirt turned rag under his hand. "Now patch me up so we can put this mud hole behind us."

Maggie worked as swiftly and competently as the cramped space allowed. When she'd finished, Court had a neat white covering over the palm of his hand.

"Thanks. Now to take off your clothes."

"What?"

"We've got hours before we reach the hospital. We're both soaked through. We need to get dry."

"Oh."

"Maggie, as desirable as I might find you, I don't think now is the time to prove it. Get changed."

She didn't have to have a mirror to know her face had gone a deep pink. She grabbed her duffel.

Court turned to check on Neetie, giving her a moment of privacy. Too soon for her comfort, he straightened in his seat and began stripping off his soggy clothes.

Maggie started the truck and put it in gear, doing her best to avert her eyes. Unable to resist any longer, she glanced at him. He'd zipped his pants but remained bare-chested. Her gaze came up to meet his. Worry still filled his blue eyes.

"I was wondering how long it would take you to look," he said drily. "We need to put some miles behind us, for Neetie's sake. Step on it."

Court woke with a start. He hadn't intended to sleep and his hand hurt like the devil, throbbing with each beat of his heart. It was almost dark outside. "How close are we to the hospital?"

"Still about six hours out. At least the rain has let up."

"Why don't you stop for a few minutes? Let's stretch our legs and I'll check on Neetie. I'll drive the rest of the way."

"A stop would be nice. I'm so cramped I don't know if I can stand." Maggie arched her back and rolled her shoulders. "How's your hand?"

"Hurts."

"I'll get you some pain-reliever when we stop."

"No, I can live without it. I don't want to take

a chance on it making me sleepy. I'll deal with it until I get to the hospital. Are you ever not in the nurse mode? Do you ever think of yourself first?"

"Sure I do."

"I bet it's not very often."

A moment went by. "Maybe not."

"That's what I thought."

"Neetie's been resting, the best I can tell. He woke long enough to eat a pack of crackers and drink some water. I reached back every so often to touch him. His temperature seems to be staying down."

Court felt some relief at that knowledge. Maybe Neetie wasn't as sick as he feared. "Yeah, but that may not last for long." Did she hear the unease in his voice?

She pulled the truck to a stop. Preparing to examine Neetie, Court pulled the blanket away. "Don't go far," Court said as Maggie climbed out.

"Remember, I'm the one that lives here."

"Yeah, but that doesn't mean you can't get lost." His protective instinct worked overtime where she was concerned. Strangely, it didn't feel wrong.

Maggie wasn't gone long, and he stood beside the driver's door, waiting for her return.

"I've been thinking," she said as she walked to him, "about what you said about getting lost. It's hard enough to find landmarks in the dry season but with the rain and darkness..." she shook her head "...I'm wondering if we should consider laying over for the night? We could get up at first light. You need to rest, take some pain meds."

"I'm all right but you know this area better than I do." Court looked off into the distance.

"We'd be safer if we stayed put. Will Neetie be okay?" Court felt more than saw her intense look.

"I don't like having to wait but it sounds as if it might be the right decision." Court ran a hand over his stubbled chin. "I'd like it even less if we slid off the road. I think we should drive until dark. Get as many miles under us as we can."

"Agreed." She seemed to be glad to have him make the call. His self-esteem ballooned.

That was quite a compliment, coming from the "let me tell you how to do it" Maggie.

"Then it's a plan," she said, climbing into the truck.

A low rumble of thunder across the expanse warned that rain was coming again soon. Court was disappointed at the amount of cumin-colored land they'd managed to cross when Maggie announced, "We need to stop while the rain has let up."

"Okay. While I check on Neetie, you see if you can move the supplies around so we'll have a place to sleep. We've had too hard a day not to lie down if we can. Get us close enough to the back of the seat so all we have to do during the night to care for Neetie is to lean over it."

"I think that's doable," Maggie said, as she found the emergency supplies she'd packed while they drove. With flashlight in her hand, she climbed out of the truck.

"Leave securing the tarp to me. I'll do that before I climb in."

As another rumble of thunder and a big fat drop of rain hit the windshield, Court checked the sky. "We might need to put a rush on settling in."

CHAPTER SEVEN

MAGGIE had managed, sometimes with difficulty, to move supplies to one side of the truck bed so there was room enough for her and Court to stretch out. A space less than a twin-size bed was better than nothing. Using two sleeping bags as padding and a couple of blankets to cover them, their quarters for the night were passable. She located the spare flashlights and switched one on.

Her heart went out to Court. He looked exhausted and pain etched his face. Even in the dim light of the cab of the truck, she'd seen the tight lines around his mouth and watched his jaw clench whenever they went over a large bump. Without an antibiotic soon, his hand would become infected. Then she'd have two acutely ill patients. Something she didn't need out in the African plain during the rainy season.

By the shift in the tarp and a knock here and there, she knew Court would soon be climbing in. Having him along made her feel safe. She would've made it without him but there was a feeling of security in having him as a partner. Checking on Neetie, she was glad to find he slept peacefully. She stayed where she was in order to give Court as much room as possible when he got in.

Court scrambled under the tarp and closed the tailgate behind him as it started to pour.

"Try not to get mud on everything." She yelled to be heard above the pounding of the rain.

"Who are you, my mother?" he called back in an agitated tone before he turned round, sat down and removed his boots.

Maggie stiffened. Had she made him mad? He'd never used that antagonistic tone with her before. It hurt to have him talk to her that way.

The space was small but Court's large body joining hers made it tinier. His shoulders hunched in the confined space as he worked with the laces of his boots. There was a thud and then another as his boots hit the metal of the floor. He began scooting backward toward her. "Do you have a towel, cloth, something I can use to dry off with?"

Without waiting for her reply, he started stripping out of his clothes. Maggie reached for her towel and handed it to him. He made a couple of ineffectual and awkward efforts using his left hand to dry himself before she took the cloth.

At his grunt of disapproval, she said, "I'll do it." She dried him the best she could, paying special attention to his hair and face before throwing the towel on a box above their heads. Court lay back and pulled the blanket to his waist.

"Here." She offered him two tablets and a water bottle. He took them and she set the bottle aside before saying, "Let me see your hand."

"Stop fussing."

"It isn't a request, Doctor, it's an order."

He held up his hand and gave her a weary smile. "I love it when you talk dirty, Nurse."

"I'm not interested in your teasing," she said in a flat tone, studying his hand. "This needs to be changed and stitched up." She pulled her bag closer and shined the flashlight into it.

"It'll wait."

"No, it won't. Sit up and hold out your good hand." She retrieved the items she needed from the bag and put them in his good hand.

"I'm putting stitches in. You shouldn't need but about eight or ten."

"What?" He tried to pull his injured hand away. "No way. Two or three, max."

She smiled. "Settle down. I was just kidding."

"You'd better be." Court relaxed his hand, letting her hold it again.

"This is going to hurt." She drew lidocaine from a vial into the syringe. "You ready?"

"Yeah."

"Sorry," she said as she inserted the needle into the skin surrounding his wound. She wished she was the one being stitched up instead of him.

"Just get on with it, Maggie."

She nodded. As she pushed the needle into his skin, he flinched and hissed but he didn't jerk away. She admired his fortitude as she made another entry. It upset her to have to hurt him.

"Maggie…"

"Uh?" She concentrated on getting it right, so she wouldn't have to hurt him any more than necessary.

"Stop biting your lip. You're going to make it bleed."

"Oh," she muttered, licking her lip, without taking her eyes away from the job at hand.

He made sound low in his throat. "And don't do that."

"What? I have to make another stitch."

"Nothing."

Minutes later she said, "There," as she tied the last small knot. "Done." She smiled at him but he didn't look as pleased as she felt. Even in the faint light he looked a little pale. "I know it hurts like heck. I did the best I could."

"Stop chattering, Maggie, and let's get some sleep."

"I don't chatter," she said in a crisp tone, securing the bandage on his hand.

"That's more like my Maggie. We need to be on the road, uh, the path, uh, whatever, by sunup."

His Maggie? When had she become his Maggie?

Her heart did a flip-flop and a river of warmth washed over her. She kind of liked the sound of that. What would it feel like to belong to Court?

Leaning across the seat, she placed a hand on Neetie. His breathing had eased and he felt cooler than he had been earlier. She flipped off the light and started to lie down.

"You're going to sleep in your clothes?" Court asked, his voice full of disbelief.

"Yes."

"No, you're not. I'm not going to have you squirming around all night, trying to get comfortable. Strip."

Her heart jumped. "I'm not going—"

"Maggie!"

By his tone of voice, she knew better than to disagree. She began to remove her clothes. Her elbow hit something hard as she pulled off her shirt.

"Turn on the light so you can see what you're doing," Court demanded, pain evident in his voice.

"No." Her stomach dipped. She wasn't doing a striptease for him.

Court grunted when her knee hit something soft while she removed her shorts.

"Woman, are you trying to kill me?"

Maggie was thankful her embarrassment didn't show under the cover of darkness. "I'm sorry, it's such a tight space."

"You know, watching you undress by flashlight would've been *the* highlight of an otherwise lousy day."

Court's rich voice with his own brand of humor sounded even sexier in the pitch dark. She tingled at the thought of his piercing blue eyes watching her undress. "Sorry, no such luck. We have to save the batteries."

"Remind me to buy extra ones for the next time we're stranded together."

"I'll put it on the list."

She lay beside him but on top of the bedroll. "What're you doing?"

"Going to sleep."

"You're going to freeze out there. Stop being silly and get under here."

"But—"

"Maggie, if you're worried about your virtue, don't be. I don't feel up to doing anything other than sleep. Come on, be a realist."

Somehow he'd managed to make her sound like a shrew. She found the edge of the blanket and flipped it back. A big hand touched her hip as she stretched out beside him before it slipped up to circle her waist. She went cold, then hot. He pulled her into position beside him, lying back to front, making his arm her pillow.

"Relax and get some sleep," he said into her ear before his lips brushed the top curve of it.

The sound of rain on the tarp enveloped them.

"Court?"

"Mmm?"

"I'm sorry I bossed you around about the mud on your boots. Force of habit."

"How's that?" His words were warm across her cheek.

She'd never explained her childhood to anyone before. Did she want Court to be the first person she told? Somehow, she believed he of all people would understand.

"My father expected my mother and me to act and look perfect. Daddy was a stickler for everything being just right. Clothes, hair, the house, the car, you name it, everything had to be just so. When it rained and I'd left muddy tracks, I was in trouble. Big trouble. Stay in my room for days trouble."

"So how did he act when people came over?"

She'd wanted friends to come by after school, have sleepovers, but her mother had always said no. Even then Maggie had dreamed of having a big family. She wasn't mad at her parents, only sad they couldn't seem to see she craved having people around her.

"That didn't happen. I always had to go to my friends' houses. Mom and I lived in fear of my father's anger and she finally reached a point she worried he might start hitting us when we weren't just as he expected."

"Now I understand why you pay such particular attention to your hair."

"Dad was always on me to keep my hair out of my face. Keep it tied back."

"I like it down. Free. It's beautiful."

A warmth she'd never experienced before filled her. "Thanks."

"That's why you're so self-reliant, isn't?" he said, giving her a gentle squeeze.

His statement hurt for some reason. "I'm not that bad, am I?"

"Yeah, but I like you anyway." His soft chuckle brushed her ear.

A burst of joy filled her even as she pushed at his arm in retaliation for his banter.

"Stop wriggling. I'm already having a hard enough time lying here with you."

She opened her mouth to respond but he growled, "Shut up, Maggie, and go to sleep."

Maggie felt Court shifting against her as he moved to check on Neetie.

"Maggie—"

She became intently alert. "What's wrong?"

"Neetie's fever has spiked. He's unconscious."

"He can't—"

"Think positive." His words were thin, slicing through her terror.

Feeling no self-consciousness, only distress over Neetie, she sat up, clicked on the flashlight and found her clothes.

Court slid to the end of the truck taking his clothes bag with him, giving her enough room to maneuver. "We need to get to Teligu ASAP. We're leaving now, dark or not. The sun should be up soon anyway." He'd jerked his clothes on and put on his boots. "I want you to get the water and find something to use as a compress. He needs to have his arms and chest bathed. We've got to bring the fever down."

Minutes later Court sat behind the steering wheel and Maggie climbed in on the other side.

Court found first gear while she located the water jug on the floor and searched through the medicine bag. She pulled out a bottle, shook out two pills and offered them to Court.

"I told you—"

"I know what you told me but I saw you flinch when you climbed into the truck and you have to use it to change gears. If you're worried about staying awake, I'll talk to you."

"I don't want them."

"Maybe so but you're going to take them anyway." She grasped the wrist of his good hand and dropped the capsules into his palm. "Take them for me, please."

In a resigned voice, he said, "Thanks. I'm going to be driving fast. Wedge yourself between the seats so you won't get hurt while seeing to Neetie. The last thing we need is for you to have a busted head."

Her hands trembled as she adjusted her body, using his shoulder for support as she got into position. Court's actions indicated his extreme concern for Neetie. "I found more liquid pain-reliever. I'm going to give him a dose."

"Good." Court slowed while she administered the liquid then he stepped on the gas.

Four hours later, after pushing the old truck for all it was worth on a muddy, rutted road, Court pulled into the hospital compound. He would've never have thought he'd be so grateful to see the simple building. He couldn't remember being this scared since his brother had died. The last few hours had taken their toll on his emotions. Despite all his knowledge of modern medicine he still couldn't make Neetie well. Like his parents hadn't been able to fix his brother's problems. There was no special machinery, no advanced medicines, no IVs, no oxygen, no...

He'd watched the boy's health slip out of his control, with no way of gaining it back unless he got Neetie to a secondary hospital in time. He also had Maggie to worry about. She didn't say it, wouldn't voice it, but she was frightened. It was killing him not be able to reassure her more.

Maggie cared for Neetie continuously but Court knew she was having a difficult time holding it together. The best he could do was to keep her from becoming more alarmed than she already was. Since when had he concerned himself with someone else's fear or worries, or emotional well-being? When had Maggie slipped under that super-max prison fence surrounding his emotions to affect him so?

She'd not kept up the constant chatter she'd promised but she'd occasionally asked if he was all right. A few times she'd touched his shoulder, and once when the rain had been beating down on them hard she'd squeezed his shoulder after he'd expressed his frustration. Those few actions helped him keep his sanity. He liked having someone show concern for him, particularly Maggie. He was used to being invisible even to his parents.

He'd only been able to glance at Maggie once in a while as he'd navigated the big lumbering truck in the dark, wet night. Her gentle crying had barely registered over the rain. She'd talked to Neetie, even though she'd gotten no response. "You're going to be fine, sweetheart. Court's going to get you to the hospital."

Court wished he had the same confidence she did. This time he might be available for a patient but it still might not save Neetie's life. Heaven help him, Neetie had become more than a patient. The kid had gotten under his skin too, just like Maggie had.

When he'd seen the primitive hospital compound ahead, relief had coursed through him. He'd blown the horn and brought the truck to a rocking stop near the building's doors. One of the orderlies had come running.

"Go get Dr. Roberts," Court snapped, opening the door of the truck and reaching in for Nettie.

"Help Missy Maggie," he called to the other orderly when Maggie had difficulty stepping out of the truck. She'd stayed on her knees, propped between the seats the entire time. Her muscles had to be nothing but knotted masses.

Court pushed his way through the hospital doors and into an examining room. Placing Neetie on a table, he said to the nurse, "I need a comp panel, def and CBC plus creatinine level. *Stat.*" The blood culture would have to wait until he got Neetie to Tema. Another facility lacking at the Teligu Hospital.

At a brush against his side, he found Maggie

reaching to take Neetie's arm. She said to Jill, "I'll draw while you get an IV started." Neetie gave an incoherent mumble as she placed the needle in his vein.

"As soon as you have the line in place, he needs a chest and abnormal X-ray," Court stated, pulling his stethoscope from his bag, which the orderly had dropped beside him.

"What's going on here?" Dr. Roberts barked.

Court gave report and stated, "I bet my plane that Neetie's enzymes are sky high. I want to fly him to Tema for an MRI when he's stable. If the damage to his liver is as extensive as I believe, he needs to go on to Boston for treatment."

Dr. Roberts nodded his head in agreement. "Thank God you were here, otherwise we could do little for the boy."

Nothing was going to stop Court from seeing this child received every medical chance available, which included Court at his side.

It was mid-afternoon before Maggie made it to her bungalow. She showered in the meager amount of warm water available in an effort to bring some life back into her cold body.

Neetie was dying. He was in the ward now, waiting for morning so Court could fly him to the coast. Unable to stand it any longer, she let go of the anguish she'd dammed behind a wall of self-control in order to do what needed to be done. In sharp gasps and heaving sobs she bent over as water poured over her back. Her child was dying. Official or not, he belonged to her.

"Maggie? Are you okay?" Court called. The painful sobbing on the other side of the thin door broke through the thick shell of uninvolvement he'd built around himself so many years ago he'd lost count of the number.

"Maggie?"

Why wouldn't she answer? He cracked the door. "Maggie?"

There was a muffled noise he couldn't make out in the water of the shower.

"Are you all right?"

Still he received no sensible answer.

"I'm coming in."

He pushed the door open. No reaction from her. "Maggie, you're scaring me. Are you okay?"

A large gulping sob filled the tiny area.

He pushed back the curtain.

"Get out. Go away."

His heart broke to see her doubled over in anguish.

"I'm not leaving you like this."

Quickly removing his boots, he stepped under the water and pulled her to him. She shifted as if to pull away but he held her tight. Maggie needed to know someone was there to support her. He couldn't be there forever but right now he could be.

She trembled in his arms but put up no further resistance to him being there. The action alone told him the depth of her fear. He pushed her sopping hair away from her face and kissed her forehead as he tried to absorb her misery. His hand cupped her head and held it against his chest. Minutes went by before Maggie limp against him as if all her restraint had disappeared. With a deep sob she wrapped her arms around him and clung as if he was her life force. Her tears mingled with the water.

He didn't want someone to depend on him as Maggie was doing, but he couldn't leave her. "Aw, Maggie, you have to stop. You're killing me. He's stable, conscious. You can't continue like this. It's not good for you."

"I'm going too," she said in halting breaths.

"I would've been surprised if you weren't. I've spoken to Dr. Roberts about you going. He okayed it."

"Thank you." Going up on tiptoe, she kissed him.

He pulled away. "Maggie, don't." Court cupped her face. "You're not thinking straight right now."

She sobered. Leaning back, she caught his wrist as if she forgotten he'd been hurt. His hand was wrapped in a neat new bandage and he wore a surgical glove over it. "I'm sorry. I forgot all about your hand."

"Don't worry about it. Dr. Roberts looked at your work and pronounced it faultless."

She kissed the skin on the inside of his wrist above the glove. He sucked in a breath. His tentative hold on his lust weakened very second he held the naked, water-slick Maggie in his arms. This good deed might kill him but he refused to take advantage of her drained emotional state.

"I couldn't have gotten Neetie here without you."

"I don't believe that," he said as he released his hold on her. "If you're going to be all right now, I think I'd better let you finish your shower and go and get mine."

"Don't go." She started pushing up his wet T-shirt. "Just need to forget for a while."

"Maggie, you don't know what you are playing at."

She placed at kiss in the center of his chest. Her tongue flicked out to taste him.

"Salty," she murmured. "Good."

"I don't want to take advantage of you."

"You need a bath and you're already here. You've got a bad hand. I can help you."

"I don't think that such a go—"

"Shut up, Doctor. I'll wash your hair then get out." She reached for the shampoo and, using the tips of her fingers, she gently scrubbed his hair.

Court couldn't resist kissing the crest of her creamy breast that was below his mouth as he bent to give her access to his head. Her sharp intake of breath made his shaft grow harder. She ran her fingers through his hair, clearing it of soap under the water. He straightened.

She blinked up at him. Worry lines still etched

her face, but anticipation, desire were there also. Leaning down, he kissed her forehead. When she made no effort to move, he kissed her temple and let his lips travel across her cheek. She turned her head, giving him an invitation to her mouth. Accepting it, he took her lips in a hungry kiss. She met him with equal appetite as he devoured her mouth. One of her hands slid along his chest, along the column of his neck to wrap around it. She tugged, bringing him nearer, crushing her lips against his as if she couldn't get enough of him. As if she'd been in limbo, waiting for an emotional release.

She moaned. His erection strained against the fly of his shorts. Court accepted her gift, encouraging her to open her mouth for him. She did. He entered. She met him, greeted him, danced with him.

Court had been hot for women before, lusted after them, but he'd never felt the burning, consuming, driving desire he felt for Maggie. She was like tinder to his combustible need. He couldn't fight it any longer. If he hadn't known Maggie needed tenderness and patience he would've turned her, taking her fast and hard. No matter what it took from him to maintain control he intend her to be caressed, pampered and reassured that she wasn't alone. For tonight. He would make no promise about tomorrow.

Maggie felt the bowstring tenseness of Court's body against her. It fed the longing deep within her. She trembled with the hunger to be a part of him, to find that perfect connection, to forget the harrowing past hours and to not think of the ones to come. To escape.

A growl she recognized as sexual needed formed low in Court's throat. A burst of heat rocketed through her. She wrapped her arms around his neck and intensified the kiss. Soon she was pushing at his wet clothing. He reached behind her, shut off the water and helped her finish the job of ridding him of shirt and pants. Placing the arm with the unhurt hand below her butt, he lifted and carried her.

"Grab a towel," he bit off, as if he was straining to hold himself in check.

Maggie snatched a towel off a hook as they went by.

Court came down on the bed with her. Taking

the towel from her, he gently dried her hair then burrowed his hands into it. He muttered, "You've no idea how many times I've stopped myself from reaching to touch your hair." He brought a handful of the mass to his mouth and kissed it before watching it trail though his fingers. "Even damp it's magnificent."

She took the towel. As she rubbed his head, he kissed her breasts. A honeyed heat built low in her.

He shifted to his back and brought her almost over him. He felt strong, sure and secure. She kissed his neck. The tips of her breasts teased his warm skin, making her tingle. Maggie squirmed, buzzing with sexual tension. She gave Court little nipping kisses along his jaw and over his cheek, her hair creating a canopy around them. They were all that existed. He ran his hand over the curve of her hip and she flexed against him. His fingertips skimmed over her until he cupped a breast.

Her eyes locked with his. They had turned dark like the sea at night and questioned as if searching for confirmation she wanted this. That he hadn't pushed her. She smiled and it grew bigger when she saw the promise in his eyes that she was enough just as she was.

He grazed the end of her nipple with his finger. "I want you like I've never wanted before," he whispered. "I won't hurt you. I only wish to give you pleasure." With two of his fingers he rolled the tip of her breast with a light touch, until it hardened.

"Please," she whispered on a fading breath, as she pressed her breast into his hand.

Court's hands moved to Maggie's waist and lifted her.

Maggie was curvy, sleek and sinuous. Heaven.

She gave to everyone, but this time he would give to her. Court positioned her so her breasts hung above him and the bulk of her hair brushed his shoulder. Slowly, he took her nipple into his mouth as if plucking a ripe grape from the vine.

Maggie shivered, and made the sweetest crooning sound. His shaft grew larger, something he would've thought impossible. She squirmed, and he moved to her other breast, giving it the same treatment, before circling his tongue around the extended nipple. He released it with a gentle tug, then blew gently over it.

Her small but determined hands captured his face and directed his mouth back to the first breast. He gave it equal devotion before he lowered her to his chest. The sensation of her silky skin against his was almost too much. He took a second to gain control. This was about Maggie.

The skin across his abdomen rippled as Maggie's fingers fluttered over it on their way downward. The tip of a finger brushed the throbbing end of his manhood. It jumped.

He flipped her, stopping further exploration. If he let her truly touch him, he might explode. His mouth sealed hers. She met him kiss for kiss. The open, responsive Maggie was almost his undoing.

She kissed his shoulder and chest. One small but purposeful hand caressed the fine hair of his torso while the other kneaded his back.

Had a woman ever acted as if she needed him more? It was a heady feeling to know that this courageous, passionate woman craved him.

Maggie placed magical kisses along the length of his neck, feathering across his collar bone. She was going to unman him if he didn't take her soon. She stopped kissing him, and looked her fill. Not normally a self-conscious man, he was a little uncomfortable under her scrutiny.

"You are so beautiful." Her eyes were filled with awe.

He reached for her. "Nowhere near as amazing as you are." He took her hand, placing a kiss in the palm. "I want you."

"I know," she said, "but it's been a long time for me."

"I thought as much."

Maggie tried to pull away but he held her close and kissed her brow. "I didn't mean that like it sounded. You don't have to have a medical degree to see there are few available men around here. And even if that wasn't the case, after what you told me..." he hesitated "...I'm not surprised you'd want to protect yourself."

Her smile was wry. "You're right.

He nudged her onto her back and gave her a wet, hot kiss. Parting her legs with a knee, he dipped a finger into her warm, slick center, while his tongue mimicked his finger in her mouth.

She arched beneath him.

Pregnancy not being a worry, he'd have the ultimate pleasure of having no barrier between them. He was climbing for the summit.

With Maggie open and ready for him, he shifted upward, found his harbor and with a slow, controlled and blissfully perfect thrust entered her. She wrapped her legs around his hips and pulled him home, meeting his thrusts as they became one. She moaned her pleasure, tensed and ground out his name before he joined her in the brilliance of oblivion.

Amid the powerful primal rhythm he found the peace he'd been so desperately searching for, the easing of the ache in his heart. A sense of empowerment. Maggie accepted him without making judgments. Recognized him for who he was. He didn't have to prove himself to her. A feeling Court couldn't identify bolted from his heart. Now it was out he feared there'd be no locking it away again.

Court lay beside her. Taking her in a possessive hold, he snuggled her against him. Enjoying the feeling of having Maggie securely in his embrace, he drifted off to sleep.

* * *

For Maggie, the past two days had been a whirl-wind Court had created and held in firm control.

She was amazed at what Court could accomplish by using the Armstrong name when he made up his mind it was the correct thing to do.

Maggie had been surprised to find Raja flying out with them. When she'd questioned Court about Raja he gave Maggie the short answer that he'd made arrangement to see about getting Raja a prosthetic leg. He didn't allow her time to find out more.

The plane ride to Tema had taken a little more than a few hours in Court's luxurious jet. An ambulance waited at the airport to whisk them away to the Provita Specialist Hospital where Neetie received an MRI and was diagnosed with hepatitis B, with primary biliary cirrhosis. Court said the diagnosis had been what he'd expected. Heartsick at the results, she was glad Court had been there to help with Neetie.

He would need a transjugular intrahepatic portosystemic shunt, or TIPS for short, if there was any chance of him surviving. The diagnosis was as bad as Maggie had feared. Where she and Neetie lived, people with hepatitis B didn't survive. The basic care given at the Teligu Hospital was too little. She was more thankful for Court than ever. Without him, Neetie wouldn't have had a chance to live. Neetie was one small example of what the Armstrong Foundation's influence could do for the people in the area around Teligu.

Throughout the days, Maggie had seen a subtle but definitive change in Court. So in tune with him from the first moment, she recognized the confidence he now had in his medical decisions. Where he'd been unsure and tentative before, he was in control and sure now.

A few hours after confirmation of Neetie's diagnosis, he was again loaded onto Court's jet and they were on their way to the States. This time Court wasn't doing all the piloting. The Armstrong Foundation had provided another pilot, giving Court the opportunity to care for Neetie, if necessary. Neetie had a comfortable spot in the plane and woke occasionally but never for long. He'd never been farther than the hospital from his village, and the plane trip alone was daunting for him. Maggie made certain she was never far away in case he called out for her.

As they flew through the darkness, Court came

into the cabin and sat down beside her. In the dim light she could see the fatigue on his face. Wrapping an arm around her shoulders, he pulled her against him and closed his eyes. "Can't sleep without you in my arms," he murmured before his even breathing told her he'd gone to sleep. She snuggled against him, took Neetie's hand in hers, closed her eyes and found rest.

Outside Boston, they boarded the helicopter that Court had arranged to have waiting. Maggie was sure the Armstrong name had something to do with the VIP treatment but Court's forceful personality had something to do with it as well. In any other circumstances Maggie would've enjoyed flying over the beautiful old city but found it another panoramic reminder of how different her and Court's lives were.

The emergency room staff was expecting them when they landed and were well organized. Maggie had been a part of almost every emergency at the Teligu Hospital but could do little more than stand aside and watch others work here. Although uncomfortable with being on the sidelines, she understood the necessity.

The paperwork was processed and Neetie was

whisked off to ICU. She and Court went up with Neetie. They were needed to translate. Maggie refused to leave his side until she was forced to by hospital rules. She held Neetie's hand and kept a constant dialogue going, as much for herself as for him. The nurses were competent and compassionate as they settled Neetie. His wary eyes focused on her regardless of what went on around him. He was so tired when he tried to speak it was little more than the puckering of his lips. Given a sedative, the boy's eyes were soon closing. As he drifted off, she whispered, "I'm right here. I love you."

Maggie wiped a tear from her cheek. She'd been devastated when the doctor had told her she couldn't have children, and if she lost Neetie…

Raja had been hurried off to somewhere unknown. Maggie never felt more out of place or out of control her life but she refused to fall apart. Court's put a hand on her waist and squeezed it encouragingly. "He'll be fine."

"He has to be. I won't let myself think differently."

"He's in one of the best hospitals in the world.

Come on, let's go and get some rest. We'll come back first thing in the morning."

"I'm staying here," she stated.

"No, you're not. You'll be no good to Neetie if you're dead on your feet. He's in good hands. Now is the time for you to take care of yourself."

Court had hoped he was wrong about Neetie's condition but there was also a feeling of exhilaration that went with knowing he'd made the right call. That old self-doubt that had plagued him for what seemed like forever began to disappear. The heavy weight he'd been carrying had lightened, making him feeling more like the doctor he'd once been.

With Neetie in the hospital ICU and the TIPS procedure planned for the next morning, Court felt better about Neetie's health than he had in days. Neetie would have a slow recovery period because of malnourishment but he was young, which was on his side.

Court observed Maggie in the late-afternoon sun while she looked out the window of the chauffeur-driven car on the way to his home.

"It's beautiful here. I've never been to Boston."

He squeezed her hand. "It is beautiful. I love this place. It has been my home all my life."

Maggie looked as him, giving him a guarded smile as they continued along the river toward the older area of the city. Had something he'd said bothered her?

A few minutes later she said, "I don't remember the name of this river."

"The Charles. During my college days I used to have crew practice along here."

"Really? We don't do much boating in northern Ghana." She continued to look out at the passing landscape.

For him, Maggie was as much a shining jewel in the green metropolis of Boston as she'd been in the drab brown of Africa. She stood out, adding life and energy to every place she went. The driver pulled the car to a stop in front of his brownstone.

"We're home." Somehow it sounded right to include Maggie in the statement.

"This is where you live?" Surprise surrounded each of her words.

"What did you expect? A big, shiny, glass-and-chrome high-rise?"

"Well, yeah, I guess I did," she said, climbing up the rock steps.

He'd told her in no uncertain terms she wouldn't be staying at a hotel near the hospital when she'd argued about staying with him. He was the emergency call number and if Neetie had any problems he would know first and so would she. Her concern for Neetie was the only reason she'd agreed to the arrangement. Maggie had made one stipulation—they would not share a bed. He wasn't pleased with the condition, but he would honor it. Despite his body's craving for hers and that it might mean days of frustration.

He unlocked the door to his home, which was over a hundred years old, and pushed it open. Maggie followed him in. He watched her as she wandered around the living room and dropped into his favorite leather chair. She wiggled into the corner and breathed deeply. She seemed to fit perfectly in his house. That was a thought he declined to examine.

"You've no idea how long it has been since I sat in a chair like this. It's almost heaven."

Court chuckled. "You keep that up and I'll be envious of a chair."

"I might like it better than I do you." She smiled at him while she rubbed her hand over the arm.

"Would you like something to eat or drink? I called my housekeeper and asked her to buy a few things."

"No, I'm fine," she murmured, laying her head back against the chair and sighing.

Court went to make some coffee anyway. He returned to find Maggie still curled in his chair but sound asleep. *Poor thing.* He smiled. Maggie would hate knowing he'd thought of her in that context. She'd been running on adrenaline for days. Terrified that Neetie wouldn't live, she'd put up a brave front more than once. She was the toughest person he knew. With Neetie stable and the procedure planned, she'd crashed.

Scooping her up, he carried her to the spare bedroom. Court enjoyed the feel of Maggie against him. She shifted but didn't wake up when he brushed his lips against hers. In such a short time she'd become precious to him. He'd not intended it to happen, had even fought against it. Was still fighting it.

What would it be like to carry her to his bed every night? Heaven. But it would never last.

* * *

The next morning Maggie found Court in the kitchen, standing by the coffeepot with nothing but his jeans on. If he ever gave up being a doctor, he needed to consider being a model. When her eyes met his, she saw mischief dancing there. "Like what you see?"

"Are there no bounds to your ego?" she huffed. "Don't we need to go? I want to be at the hospital before Neetie wakes up. I know he's terrified. He's never seen anything like the hospital."

"We'll be there in plenty of time. He's been so sick I'm sure he's sleeping."

"Still—"

"I know. Little Miss Mama needs to see about her chick."

She bowed her back. "Yes, I do, and if you're not ready I'll call a taxi."

"Ho, that's not necessary. Give me a sec to finish dressing."

Maggie prepared a cup of tea while she waited. She'd missed having Court next to her during the night. She'd woken a number of times searching for him, only to curl into a ball and dream of his touch again. It had to be this way, otherwise she'd leave her heart behind in Boston when she left.

Neetie was awake when she and Court went to his bedside. Maggie flicked Court an "I told you so" look. The whites of Neetie's eyes were still a hazy yellow. Thankfully his fever was almost gone. After the TIPS procedure he should recover quickly. She looked forward to having the old talkative Neetie back. Maggie smiled. She missed his jabber, even though she had to tell him to hush way too often.

A couple of nurses arrived to take Neetie down to the radiology department to do the TIPS. "Come on, I think they'll let us walk down with him," Court said.

"Sure, Dr. Armstrong. That should be fine," one of the nurses said, looking at Court as if he were cake and it was her birthday. For the first time in her life Maggie wanted to put a sign on a man that read "Mine." No matter what had passed between Court and herself earlier, she had no right to think that way.

Court paid the nurse no attention. Instead, he concentrated on walking beside her while she held Neetie's hand.

"The parents' waiting room is just off this hallway," the other nurse directed.

The statement took her by surprise. Her and Court parents? Neetie's parents? She did like the sound of it, though. "We're not his... I'm going to—"

Court caught her hand for a second. "She's letting us know where the waiting room is. Not making legal pronouncements."

"Yeah, uh, I know," she mumbled, intrigued by the prospect that she and Court could share parenthood. No, it would never work. He'd even told her they had no future.

"Come on, I'll buy you breakfast while Neetie's having the procedure. That way you can concentrate on your food instead of worrying for a while."

They left Neetie and walked to the cafeteria. "You don't have to be at the foundation?" Maggie asked Court.

"Nope, I have no intention of leaving you here by yourself. This is one time you don't have to do it alone."

"Thanks." She meant it.

The day went by faster than Maggie had expected. After the hepatologist announced Neetie had come through the procedure like a champ, she spent the rest of the day sitting beside his bed. Normally he would've gone to the step-down unit but Neetie had been so sick before the procedure that his doctor wanted to err on the side of caution and keep him in ICU another night. Neetie would go to the step-down floor the next day if he remained stable during the night.

Court left to check in at the foundation an hour after Neetie had returned to the ICU. Maggie hadn't realized how much she missed Court until he'd gone but even worse was the realization of how dependent she'd become on him.

They were a great team in medical situations, and they had worked well together when they'd been stuck. With Neetie's care, they'd both done what had been necessary to save the boy's life. She'd never shared the kind of connection with another person, on all levels, that she shared with Court. She'd miss him when she and Neetie returned to Africa.

For years she'd worked at being self-sufficient, always making the decisions, taking care of the task on her own. Trying to make things be just right. But during the past few days she'd had to bow to Court on decisions. She found she liked having someone besides herself to lead in a crisis. It had been comforting to have him shoulder some of the burden.

Still, her world was Ghana and he said nothing about wanting her.

CHAPTER EIGHT

THAT evening, Court insisted Maggie leave the hospital as soon as visiting hours were over. He suggested they go to a restaurant but Maggie said she wasn't interested in a big meal and would rather have a sandwich at home.

The amount of time they were spending alone at his place was starting to grate on his nerves. There was a comfort he'd never known to having Maggie around to come home to while at the same time he wouldn't let himself get used to it. He was only helping her because of Neetie. For no other reason.

While he made some calls in his office, Maggie was supposed to be watching TV. Instead, he found her in front of the tall bookshelf where a few causal pictures of his family stood. His housekeeper had placed them after he'd left them piled on a shelf. He'd not bothered to remove them.

"Would you tell me about the people in these

pictures?" She pointed to one full of women and children.

"Those are my sisters. All three of them with their children. Eight between them."

"They look happy."

"I guess they are. I don't see them much. The picture was a Christmas present one year."

"They don't live close?"

"No, they all live here in town."

"If I had that many nieces and nephews I'd make sure I was the aunt they all wanted to visit."

"I don't doubt that. And you would be too."

"The holidays must be a lot fun with such a large family."

"I wouldn't know. I'm always off snow skiing during that time."

"And I thought my holidays were kind of sad."

"How's that?"

"They're usually quiet affairs. But now I'm going to have Neetie I'll make sure they are more festive, maybe cook for the staff. See if my mother would come for a visit." She sounded so happy. He liked knowing he'd had a part in making her feeling that way.

She picked up another picture. "How old were you when this was taken?"

"Around sixteen."

"You weren't bad looking even then." She bent over to get a closer look.

"Are you saying you think I'm good looking now?" He cocked an eyebrow.

"I think you know you are."

"It would be nice to hear it coming from you."

She ignored that statement and pointed to a small picture. "What about this one?"

He wished he'd steered her away from the pictures before now. "Five."

She glanced at him. Had she heard the sadness in his voice? The picture was of his family. "Which one is you?"

Maggie didn't say anything, just waited for him to fill in the huge, vacant questioning space between them. Court picked up the framed picture, studied it. "That's me…" he pointed to the little boy standing beside his mother but not touching her "…and that was my twin brother, Lyland, sitting in my mother's lap."

It wasn't a subject he discussed with even his family. It was a part of the iceberg of guilt that needed to remain under the water. He'd been jealous of his disabled brother. Had wanted some of the attention. Enough so that he'd caused trouble and had been sent to boarding school. But for some reason he wanted Maggie to know about Lyland. "It was taken a long time ago."

She took the picture from him, ran her finger over the face of the little boy he had been. "It had to have been hard to lose your brother. Especially a twin."

"It was. He was the other part of me. But in many ways he was already lost to me." His family never talked about Lyland. The pain was so solid even so many years later.

Maggie cocked her head in question, and returned the picture to the shelf before picking up another one. This time it was a picture of him looking solemn as if he carried a boulder-size burden on his young shoulders.

"That's me on my ninth birthday. It would've been Lyland's also but he had died the week before," he said drily.

Not even her sharp intake of breath made him look down at her. He didn't want to see the pity in her eyes.

Maggie placed the picture back on the shelf, turned, wrapped her arms around his middle and hugged him tightly. "I'm sorry. So sorry."

His chest tightened like it had the day his father had come to his boarding school to tell him that Lyland was dead. He'd learned early in life that if you didn't care then you wouldn't hurt. But it had been impossible to shut the guilt out the next morning after the gala when he'd found out about his friend's child and the fear he'd experienced when he'd realized how deathly ill Neetie was and that he might not be able to save him in time. His close-your-heart-off motto had served him well until Maggie and Neetie had entered his life. Somehow having Maggie around eased the blame, which never disappeared totally except when he was with her.

"Will you tell me what happened?" she asked against his chest.

"Mother and Daddy have always loved to travel. During their trips they became more and more concerned about the living conditions of the countries they visited. That's when they convinced my great-grandfather to start the foundation. They were working in Yemen when Mother started having trouble. She had no idea that she was having twins, she just knew that the baby was coming early."

He took a halting breath and Maggie gave him an encouraging squeeze. "I was born first, Lyland came a while later. There were complications. With no real medical facilities near, Lyland suffered brain damage. He required special care all his life. Mother and Daddy pretty much devoted their lives to him. He died of pneumonia because he couldn't move around enough to keep his lungs clear."

"I can't imagine how hard that was for you."

He didn't say anything.

"You were lonely after he died and no one noticed, did they?" The words were less of a question and more of a statement. She understood him. No one, not even his parents, had ever realized how alone he felt.

"Part of the reason I became a doctor was to help children like Lyland. Instead, I made the wrong call and caused another child to be like him."

The dampness on his shirt let him know that Maggie was crying. For him.

The crack in this emotional shell grew larger. His strong, stalwart Maggie was crying for him, and the little boy he'd been. His chest tightened, and agony like he'd never known swamped him. She would be leaving him just like all the others.

Her arms went slack around him, as she pulled away enough to look him in the eyes. "For a smart, worldly-wise man, you should know better than anyone that you can't control everything." She cupped his cheek. "You've got to stop beating yourself up over things you can't change, things that happened in the past or that you don't have a say in."

Maggie was thrilled when Neetie was released from the hospital the next morning. He would need to have a follow-up visit in the doctor's office in a week. She, Neetie and Court visited Raja before they left the building. Maggie was equally tickled with how well she was doing as she practiced with her new leg. Raja had a smile on her face as she demonstrated what she'd learned. Court might try not to be emotionally attached to his patients but he failed miserably with Raja and Neetie because his actions demonstrated something wholly different.

She and Neetie would be staying at Court's. He'd shot down the idea of them finding a hotel in no uncertain terms when she'd suggested that they might be in his way. Maggie hadn't really wanted to go elsewhere. Soon she and Neetie would have to leave. Knowing that day was coming, she wanted to spend as much time with Court as possible.

Every night she spent down the hall in her own bed away from Court was anguish. She couldn't count the number of times she'd thought about going to him, had relived those precious hours she'd been in his arms. Did Court want her as much as she did him?

Maggie unlocked the door to Court's brownstone while he carried Neetie up the steps. "Wow," she said, as Neetie pierced the quiet room with a yelp of delight. There was a tub of toys sitting in the middle of the room.

"Down." Neetie wiggled to get out of Court's arms.

"Where did you get these?" Maggie asked.

"I asked one my sisters."

Maggie grinned at his sheepish look.

"I guess she was so surprised to hear from me she called the others. Neetie seems to be happy."

With a wide-eyed look of wonder the boy pulled toys out of the tub and placed them on the floor.

She gave Court a hug. "To my knowledge, he's never owned a real toy." She blinked, trying to stop the moisture from forming in her eyes. "I don't want him to get too used to this. It isn't real life for him."

Court hugged her close. "Ah, honey, let him enjoy. You worry too much. He can take one or two back with him. Surely that won't hurt."

"Your heart isn't all that small either." She looked at him. "I which I could do more for all the kids like Neetie."

He stepped back and frowned. "Like getting support from the foundation?"

"Yes. I haven't forgotten about needing the foundation's help."

"I really didn't think for a minute you had." For some reason he sounded displeased with her. It saddened Maggie to know that he still didn't readily agree about the grant issue. He'd more than seen first hand the need.

"Look, Mister Doctor," Neetie held up an action figure up with a proud look on his face.

Court sat down on the floor beside the boy.

"You're spoiling him. It'll be hard for him to go home," Maggie complained. "He's already on a culture shock high."

Court presented his sexy grin that always made her give in as he pulled a toy out of the box.

Neither Court nor Neetie paid her any attention as they put their heads together and made fighting sounds. This was the kind of moment she'd always hoped to share with her own little family. So perfect was the bubble it had to burst, and this time it would hurt so deeply she'd never be able to run away from it. Nothing would ever feel right again.

Neetie had been home a few days and felt so much better he'd become stir crazy. Court came home early and told Maggie he wanted to take Neetie somewhere, just the two of them, to give her some time to herself. Maggie took him up on the offer.

"How about dropping me off at the nearest mall? I promised myself that the next time I got to the States I'd have a pedicure and manicure. I thought I'd do a little shopping also. I'll get a taxi back."

At the mall entrance, Court gave her a quick kiss. Something he did any time she gave him an opening to do so. He missed having her in his arms, above all in his bed. He took what little he could when he got a chance and was always left wanting more.

"We'll go out to dinner so don't worry about fixing anything if you beat us home."

"Sounds nice. Court..." she grabbed his arm "...don't let Neetie overdo it."

"Don't worry, I'll take care of him. You have a good time."

Thirty minutes later when he pulled his car into a parking spot in the large asphalt lot he wondered if he'd actually known what he'd been saying when he'd given Maggie that last reassurance. What did he know about caring for a child? Not the medical side, but about making an emotional investment. He'd never even babysat his nieces or nephews. "We're here."

Neetie looked at him with unsure eyes. "Where is here?" he asked in Mamprusi.

"The zoo."

"Zoo. I not know zoo."

"Come on, buddy, I'll show you. I think you'll like it."

As they strolled toward the gate, Neetie slipped

his hand into Court's. At first the trust the gesture implied made Court nervous but he discovered he liked it that the boy had faith in him.

Inside the zoo, the first animals they visited were the elephants. Neetie laughed as the large animals threw water on their backs. Impatient, Neetie soon pulled on Court's hand. He was ready to see more. They made their way to the snake house, where Neetie stood behind Court's legs the moment he saw the first large snake.

"Look." Court touched the glass of the cage. "They can't hurt you." After that Neetie slipped out from behind Court's legs but even then he stood close enough that he touched Court. "Don't worry, I won't let anything happen to you." Those words Court had never thought he'd say to another person, let alone to a child. For the first time Court understood how Roger must've felt when he'd found out about Jimmy having brain damage.

"Not like. Hurt," Neetie said, bringing Court out of his dismal thoughts.

"How about we go see the bears?" Neetie agreed but by the perplexed look on his face Court could tell he had no idea what Court was talking about. He took it for granted the boy would know what a bear was when in reality he'd never been given an opportunity to see one. Court wanted more for Neetie and with Maggie he would have that chance. But what about the other children in Ghana? Could he do more? Would the foundation?

Neetie loved the polar bears. Only by enticing Neetie away with talk of a hot dog did he get Neetie to leave.

Court laughed when Neetie screwed up his face at the taste of mustard.

"I want more," Neetie said, after finishing the hot dog.

"I don't think Missy Maggie would like it if I brought you home sick. How about we go see the monkeys instead?"

Neetie was just as fascinated with the monkeys. Court had been to the zoo a number of times as a very young child but he couldn't remember having as much fun seeing the animals as he was seeing them through Neetie's eyes. Court was having fun. He wished Maggie had come with them. They would have to bring her next time.

But she and Neetie were leaving soon. He didn't want to examine why that thought bothered him so much.

Neetie tugged at his shirt. "Restroom."

"Okay, let's find one." Minutes later, Court stood outside a stall, waiting. He'd seen fathers doing the same thing but Court would've argued that he'd never be caught doing it. His life had certainly made a major turn.

"I done," Neetie said, coming out of the stall.

"Be sure to wash your hands," Court said. He didn't recognize himself any more. He'd even started sounding like a parent.

They spent the next couple of hours seeing the rest of the animals. As they were making their way back to the car, Neetie began to lag behind. "How about a piggy-back ride?"

"I not want pig on back."

Court laughed. "I'll show you." He bent down. "Get on my back. Put your arms tight around my neck. That's it." Court put his arms under the boy's legs and shifted him upward.

"How's that?"

"I like being pig on back"

Court chuckled. He liked Neetie being *pig on back* also. What Court didn't like was that this might be the last time the two of them took a piggy-back ride. "Hold on tight."

Neetie was strapped in and Court was closing the car door when Neetie looked at Court with sleepy eyes and said, "I like you, Mister Doctor."

Court's heart contracted. Now he knew what it was like to have a child look at you with complete devotion. Court rubbed his head. "I like you too."

Maggie had spent the better part of the afternoon being pampered. She'd almost forgotten how nice it was to do something for herself. When she arrived home, Court and Neetie were not there.

When the doorbell rang she thought it must be Neetie playing with it again. He had discovered the bell the day before and found it fascinating. She opened the door to find a statuesque woman in her sixties. Maggie had no doubt this older female version of Court was his mother.

"Hello, I'm Grace Armstrong. And you must be Maggie."

"Yes. Court isn't at home right now."

"You are who I wanted to see. May I come in?"

"Oh, yes, I'm sorry. Do." Maggie opened the door wider and allowed her entrance. Where was Court and why didn't he come on home? "Um, would you like a cup of tea?"

"That would be lovely."

Maggie was even more disconcerted when Court's mother followed her into the kitchen. She was dressed in tailored slacks with a simple blouse that screamed expensive. In a graceful movement she sat in one of the chairs at the table.

"When I got a phone call from my daughter telling me that Court had a woman and child staying with him I had to come and see for myself."

"Mrs. Armstrong—"

"Please, call me Grace." It was a demand instead of a request. Maggie didn't have to use her imagination to know where Court's forceful personally had originated.

"So tell me what's going on between you and my son."

Every muscle in Maggie drew tight. What was Court's mother up to? Maggie's hand shook as she placed the tea cup on the table in front of the woman.

Grace smiled, reached over and patted her arm. "I'm a prying mother who wants to know what's going on with her son."

"We're coworkers. I'm a nurse at the hospital in Teligu, Ghana, West Africa. I'm only here because a boy from one of the villages needed surgery and I came to see about him."

"Well, I think there may be more to it than that. To my knowledge, no woman has ever stayed at Court's home. It's his sanctuary."

"Court has been very kind to Neetie and me."

Grace gave her a knowing smile then said, "Tell me about where you live and what you do."

Maggie was much happier with this subject. She described the hospital and the people in Northern Ghana. With Grace's encouragement, Maggie even shared her plans for outlying clinics.

"You sound every devoted to your work."

"It's my life. I love the people. But they have to struggle for good medical care." Maggie hesitated. "Did you know that the hospital submitted an application for a grant to the Armstrong Foundation?"

"Yes. Court mentioned it at a board meeting."

So if it hadn't been for his sister and the foundation Court's mother would've had no idea about her. Still, this could be Maggie's chance to sway someone on the board to her way of thinking. "I wish the foundation would reconsider it."

The front door opening and Court calling, "Maggie!" ended their conversation.

"I'm in the kitchen with your mother." Maggie watched Court's mother stiffen.

Neetie came bounding into the room. "Missy Maggie, we saw big lion. A bear. Birds."

Court followed. He always took her breath away when she looked at him. Neetie continued to jabber on about animals and she looked at Court questioningly.

"We've spent the afternoon at the zoo. You're getting a rundown of every animal he saw."

Maggie gave Neetie a hug. "So I guess you had a big day."

Neetie nodded vigorously but stopped short when he realized someone else was in the room.

"Neetie, this is Mister Doctor's mother," Maggie said, and then gave him a nudge and said, "Why don't you go and play?" He hopped out the door.

"Mother," Court said with a curt nod. His smile faded and a farrow creased his forehead.

"Courtland."

Where was the kiss or hug that should have been there between mother and son?

"Why are you here?" Court asked.

Maggie's eyes widened. "Court, she came to see me. She wanted to know about Ghana."

"I thought I'd come by and meet the young lady staying with you since I knew you wouldn't be bringing her to the house to meet your father and me."

"Really, Mother? You've never shown any interest in my friends before."

What was wrong with him? Maggie had never seen Court act so callously toward anyone. "Court, why don't you sit and I'll fix you a cup of tea."

"I don't care for one. Are you ready to go to dinner?"

Court's mother stood, gripping her clutch purse. "I'll be going."

"I'll show you out," Court said, already heading to the front door.

"Maggie, it was a pleasure to meet you. Please forgive my son's lack of manners," Grace said.

Maggie watched from the kitchen door as Court followed his mother outside. When he returned he looked more agitated than he had been earlier. "Are you okay?"

"I'm fine. Leave it alone, Maggie. This isn't something you can fix."

CHAPTER NINE

AT HOME again after their dinner out, Maggie put a tired Neetie to bed. He'd been quieter than usual as they'd driven home and he didn't seem to be as excited about his supper as she had expected him to be.

"He's doing fine but we'll keep checking on him regularly, don't worry," Court said when she voiced her concern. His good humor had returned by the time they had arrived at the restaurant. "Now, how about taking care of me?" He gave her a wolfish grin. "I need these stitches out." At what had to have been her surprised look, he laughed. "Well, I guess I know where your mind was."

"Don't flatter yourself, Doctor," Maggie said with a huff as she left to find her suture removal kit.

As she worked at taking out the stitches in his hand, he aggravated her by blowing in her ear. Finished, she couldn't help but glow under his praise in regard to what a fine job she'd done of sewing him up. She stood from where she'd been sitting on the footstool, planning to put her kit away, but Court caught her hand and pulled her onto his lap.

"Leave it. I want to say thank you." His lips came down on hers.

Unable to resist, Maggie wrapped her arms around his neck and gave herself up to the sweet sensation of being in Court's embrace. It would be moments like this that she would miss when she went home.

Court's hand slipped under her top and covered her left breast, sending a burst of heat to her center. If she didn't stop him now, she'd never be able to. Heartache lay down that path. She'd had enough of that in the past to last a lifetime. Maggie pushed against his shoulder. Court groaned his displeasure.

"I need to check on Neetie," she said, climbing off Court's lap, leaving him complaining about knowing how to mistreat a man.

Maggie had a gut feeling something wasn't right with Neetie. She was pleased to find he wasn't running a fever. Occasionally the boy groaned in his sleep but didn't wake up. Yawning, Maggie lay down on the other twin-size bed and pulled a crocheted coverlet over her. She'd rest her eyes for a minute before she checked on Neetie again.

A swoosh of cool air hitting her skin awakened her. She was being lifted in strong arms she recognized and cradled against a firm chest. *Court.*

"What're you doing?"

"Hush, you'll wake Neetie."

"Is something wrong? Let me down. I need to check on Neetie."

"Yeah, there's something wrong," he grumbled. "You belong in my bed." He nudged his bedroom door closed before placing her on the bed. "I checked Neetie. He's fine."

"You can't just—"

He placed a soft kiss on her lips. "Hush. You're leaving soon." His hand cupped her breast, caressed it as if he had all the time in the world. "I need you."

His sweet, beseeching words tore at her heart. She reached up and brought his head down to hers, kissing him with all the love and caring she felt but knowing this couldn't last. "I need you too."

Their lovemaking was the most poignant Maggie had ever experienced. Court was tender and caring, bringing her high and holding her there until she tumbled over onto a blissful cloud, before he started all over again. He couldn't seem to get enough of her. It was as if he wanted to memorize every nuance of her and brand his mark on her so that no other man could replace him. Their union had been slow, easy and stimulating, as if they were both grasping for something they couldn't hold on to. Instead, it had her in its grip—she was hopelessly in love.

In the early hours of the morning Maggie slipped from under the heavy arm holding her, and then from the sheet. Court grumbled, rolled over and reached out as if hunting for her before settling again. Maggie pulled Court's shirt over her head and padded down the hall on bare feet.

As soon as she entered Neetie's room she knew something was wrong. Neetie was too still.

"Court!" she yelled at the top of her lungs.

He hurried into the room, wearing nothing but his boxers. "What's wrong?"

"Neetie. Something's wrong." She'd already

pulled the covers back. "Neetie, can you hear me?" She shook him.

"I'll get my bag," Court said shortly, and left.

Going to the bathroom, she wet a cloth and started bathing Neetie's face. She couldn't swallow the lump of despair in her throat. He barely opened his eyes. Was she going to have to relive those days of panic and fear all over again?

Court returned and examined Neetie. "He needs to go to the hospital. You get his stuff together. He'll need to be admitted. I'll get dressed." There were no words of reassurance for her, just crisp doctors' orders.

While Court loaded Neetie, she dressed and stuffed her belongings into her bag. She grabbed up both bags and was out the door in record time.

The trip to the hospital was little more than a fast-forward nightmare. Maggie sat in the backseat, holding the limp Neetie as Court steered the car through the quiet streets, all the while talking on his cellphone at the same rapid pace. With a squeal of tires he pulled into the circular drive of the emergency entrance of the hospital.

The hospital staff came running to meet them. Neetie was lifted from her arms. Court stayed close to the gurney, leaving Maggie to follow behind.

She sat in an uncomfortable plastic chair and Court stood against the wall as they waited on the results from a battery of bloodwork and X-rays. She shivered more from fear than cold. Wrapping her arms around her middle, she wished Court would hold her, reassure her. Instead, he was on the other side of the tiny room with his arms folded tight across his chest. He was more remote than she'd even seen him. She wondered if he was beating himself up inside about Neetie's relapse but he could have been on the other side of the world for the amount of emotion he showed. It was as if he had gone to a place where she couldn't reach him.

Joy filled her when Neetie came to moments after being wheeled back into the room. He opened his eyes briefly as he lay on the gurney between her and Court.

"Honey, you'll be better soon. Eating ice cream again." She kissed him.

Neetie's doctor entered the room.

Maggie jumped up and faced the doctor. "What's wrong with him?"

"Neetie's experienced hepatic encephalopathy. It's sometimes a complication to the TIPS procedure. We think a toxic product from the intestines that is normally removed by the liver went to the brain. This can cause a range of brain issues from mild memory loss to a coma."

Maggie saw Court stiffen. There couldn't have been a more devastating diagnosis for Court to hear. Was he reliving his experience with Jimmy and his brother all over again?

"Thankfully it seems to have been caught early. With care and a few days in the hospital Neetie should be fine. He's young enough that if he has any complications he should outgrow them."

As soon as the doctor left Court said without looking at her, "I'll stay until Neetie gets in a room but then I'll need to go. I have a meeting at the foundation this morning."

The emotionally removed doctor she'd known during those first few days he'd been in Teligu had returned with a vengeance. He'd not touched Neetie since they'd left the house. Even now he couldn't seem to make eye contact with her, much less the boy.

"Why don't you go on? We'll be fine," Maggie said, working to keep the hurt out of her voice.

"Are you sure?"

The words were said so dispassionately she knew he was only being polite. "I'm sure."

Court gave her a curt nod and was gone.

Had they really been in bed together just hours earlier? Had the emotional bond she thought they shared been a lie? Had she once again misread a man's feelings? She had the sudden urge to throw something, to stomp her feet, to shake some sense into Court.

By the time the sun set, Neetie was still not feeling well enough to eat, but his doctor said he was improving. The plan was to watch Neetie a few more days and then he could be discharged. Maggie asked if he could go home to Ghana—after all, Court had made it perfectly clear there was no life for them together in Boston. When Neetie's doctor hesitated she explained she was a nurse and Neetie would be living with her. The doctor gave his halfhearted consent.

Neetie had been in the hospital for two days and Court hadn't visited even once. He'd made a short impersonal call asking about Neetie but nothing more. As attentive and considerate as Court had been when transporting Neetie to help from Ghana and later after surgery, he seemed to have deserted them now. What was going on with him? Had his concern over Neetie dying choked off his emotions?

Maggie tried to make excuses, but she couldn't find a satisfactory one. She was hurt and Neetie was too.

Late that evening, Maggie looked up when the door opened from where she made her bed on the plastic window seat. Court stood in the artificial light from the hallway.

"Hey," she said. He looked like he'd rather be anywhere else but there. Could her heart break more?

Court wore no smile and seemed reluctant to enter the room, as if he'd come to see them out of obligation instead of true concern. Could he turn his feelings on and off so rapidly? Did nothing that had happened between them matter? The more Maggie thought about his actions, the more annoyed she became. She'd stewed for days, and now she was ready to boil.

"How is he?" Court closed the door behind him, but didn't move any closer or look at the sleeping Neetie.

"The doctor says he'll be well enough to go home tomorrow. You'd know that if you'd come around." The statement was petty but she couldn't resist saying it. She wanted to shake him out of his self-imposed one-person world.

"I've had pressing foundation business."

"Right. Who are you trying to fool? You can't even look at Neetie. You even showed up after his bedtime. Had you hoped I would be asleep also so that way you wouldn't have to speak to us?" Court just looked at her. The fact he didn't argue the point telling in itself. With a huff of disgust she asked, "Do you even care?"

"Maggie, that isn't fair. Of course I care."

"You've a funny way of showing it. So please don't stay if it's too difficult. You're only here to appease your conscience anyway."

He shifted on his feet as if the shot had hit its mark. "I don't know what you're talking—"

"Oh, come on, Court. You exited our lives the other night. I know this is too close for comfort for you." He blanched. She'd read him correctly. He was running scared.

"I don't know what you mean."

"I think you do. You care but you don't want to." She waited until his look met hers. "You need to know that you haven't failed Neetie or me."

"I never thought I had."

"Really? That's not true from what I've seen. You left your practice because you thought you'd failed a patient." When he started to speak she held up a hand. She couldn't resist giving him both barrels. "I've watched you care for people in Teligu, in the village and most of all with Raja and Neetie. Court, you have a gift. A gift that shouldn't be wasted. Your kind of compassion and caring—when you let go and allow yourself to show it—not everyone has. You're a brilliant doctor who won't let himself practice. In that area, yes, you are failing."

"You don't understand."

"I think you're wrong there also. I understand better than most. I know what it's like to feel like a failure. My ex-fiancé had me believing I was one. What I learned is that sometimes you have to stop running and face what is chasing you."

"This isn't about you and Neetie."

"You're right. It's about you. Neetie and I need someone who can commit for the long haul. Who cares enough to take a chance on us. From what I've seen, you can't trust yourself to do that."

"How I feel isn't your business."

"You've made that clear. But you have been, until recently, a good friend. I care enough to be a friend in return. That's what I'm trying to be. It'll be your fault if you don't start doing what you should be doing, what makes you who you are, makes you happy. You can't control everything. It wasn't your fault your brother died or that your parents treated you like you didn't exist. It wasn't your fault that a patient had a reaction to medicine. And it certainly isn't your fault Neetie got sick again."

"No one is perfect, Maggie." Court couldn't help but go on the defensive. Maggie was the queen of fix-it. Make it perfect. Just like her father had wanted it. That's how he'd ended up going to Ghana in the first place—because she was trying to fix the hospital. "I can't be fixed, not even by you."

"I don't want to fix you. I want you to do it for

yourself, because you need to do it. Carrying guilt or whatever is keeping you emotionally distant from people will never let you truly live life. I'm tired of trying to find the perfect life. I'm going to start building the best life I can. And you should too."

Maggie was right but he refused to admit it to himself or to her out loud. "You have it all figured out, don't you?" The words came out as if he'd bitten into something unpleasant. He was starting to dislike himself even more, if that was possible. He wanted to punch something. More than that, he wanted not to care. For it not to hurt so badly.

"Missy Maggie knows best."

"No, I don't, but what I do know is that if you don't face your problems you're going to end up a sad, lonely man with regrets. That will be such a waste."

"Well, it must be nice to have it all figured out."

Her head jerked back as if she'd been slapped. "I ran once too. But I've stopped. I've found my place in Ghana. Where I belong. *Found you*. I found Neetie. I see a future there. I'm building that future. You're stuck in the past. You can't even carry on a civil conversation with your parents. You can't face your best friend. You shut people out. You care but you refuse to admit it. Now you're doing the same to Neetie and me."

Court stood with his legs apart, facing her. He took a deep breath. "You can't take care of everyone, Maggie. Can't make everything okay for everyone. You can't save us all!"

"You don't want to be saved! You want to wallow in your misery and resentment. At least I'm using my gifts to help people who need it. I've accepted who I am and now I have Neetie to build a family with. I'm taking a different fork in the road. I'm choosing to stop running, to be happy. Are you ever going to do that?"

The words hung heavy and dark between them. Court glared at her, angry at her words and angry at himself. Knowing the fear of one day losing Maggie or Neetie held him immobile. Instead of unending agony later, he would let them go now.

Maggie broke the silence between them. "I've made arrangements for a flight to Ghana. We're leaving straight from here tomorrow."

His eyebrows rose. "I could have the foundation—"

"You've done enough. I've already taken care of everything."

"Then I'll drive you to the airport."

"Do you really want to do that, Court? You'd have to be closed up in a car with us."

"I'll be here tomorrow to take you and Neetie to the airport," he snapped. He left, closing the door with a final click behind him. Who was Maggie to tell him what he needed to do? Or how he felt?

Court didn't sleep much that night. He spent most of it sitting in his chair, reliving the sting of every word Maggie had thrown at him. Was she right? Was he choosing to act like a failure? Was he letting his parents' decisions years ago rule his life?

The sun was rising when Court gave in to the nagging voice that said Maggie was right. He had demons he needed to shake off, put behind him. The satisfaction of practicing medicine had returned while he'd been in Ghana. Despite the fears he had for Neetie, Court's confidence had grown as he'd done what had been necessary to save the boy's life. If he was to move past his guilt and continue in his profession then he had to speak to Roger, see how Jimmy was doing.

But the fear that held him in its grip was that if he put himself out there, admitted he cared for Maggie and Neetie, he'd be opening himself up to possible pain. He loved Lyland and he was gone. His parents hadn't died but they had been just as lost to him as Lyland. What if he lost Maggie or Neetie? Giving his heart to them meant that he might experience all that agony again. No, he couldn't live through that.

As soon as it was reasonable to do so, he punched in Roger's home number. After Court explained who he was, the housekeeper told him Roger had taken Jimmy to the hospital for his physical therapy appointment. Were the fates controlling his life? Maybe Maggie's influence of "caring for everyone" extended to realigning the universe so that the signs pointed him in the correct direction. Or maybe it was the way it should be. Whatever it was, he would speak to Roger before he took Maggie and Neetie to the airport.

Court took a deep breath and pushed open the glass doors to the physical therapy department. A bitter taste filled his mouth. It suddenly seemed warmer than it should have been in the small waiting room. He found Roger sitting in one of the chairs against the wall. Roger looked up from the papers in his hand.

"Court, what are you doing here?" Roger remained seated.

Court walked toward him as his belly drew into a knot. "I came to speak to you. I want to tell you how sorry I am."

"Why now, Court? Where have you been for the past six months?"

Shame washed over Court. "I should've been there for you. For Jimmy and Alice."

Roger stood. "We know there was nothing you could have done, but as a friend and Jimmy's doctor we thought you would have at least come to the hospital."

"I don't have an excuse that will ever justify my actions in your eyes or mine. All I can say is that I'm sorry, so sorry. How's Jimmy doing?" The question was for Roger but Court looked at the boy coming toward them.

When Jimmy stopped beside Roger he put his arm across the boy's shoulders.

"Well enough. He's getting the therapy he needs and is improving. We have a new normal, but he's a happy boy." Roger's smile was one of unconditional love as he looked at his son.

The boy gave his father a lopsided smile much like the one Neetie had given Court when they'd visited the zoo. Because of Neetie Court had a better sense of how Roger felt about his son.

Jimmy pulled on Roger's hand. "We've got to go. I promised Jimmy ice cream if he worked hard."

"Roger," Court called, halting Roger's departure. When he turned Court held his friend's gaze. "Perhaps I could call round…some time."

Court held his breath as his oldest and closest friend assessed him with a level look. Finally, after what felt like an age, Roger nodded, a small smile lifting the corners of his lips.

Court nodded in return, then watched father and son leave. The impossibly heavy weight of remorse he carried hadn't disappeared but it had begun to ease.

By the time Court arrived to pick them up, Maggie's emotions were already stretched to the limit and were taking a double beating. Neetie, who was usually a willing soul, balked at everything she asked him to do.

Packing and preparing to leave was a subdued undertaking. She didn't know if she would make it to the plane before breaking down. As difficult as leaving Court was, it was still the right thing to do. She and Neetie had become too attached to him. This time she wasn't running to Ghana, this time she was going home, but she was leaving part of her heart behind.

Maggie wished Court hadn't insisted on taking them to the airport. They needed a clean break and prolonging their goodbye wasn't making it easier on her or Neetie. Neither she nor Court spoke outside necessary conversation as he made his way through the mid-morning traffic. It wasn't the comfortable kind of quiet that they had experienced before but one with an air of resignation, despondency and the desire to say something that could stop the forward motion of what was about to happen. Neetie was oddly silent, as if he sensed the raw tension between her and Court.

Maggie bit her lip and gripped the doorhandle. The confined quarters of the car were closing in on her. Getting out was all she could think about.

Her hands started to shake. She knotted them in her lap. She looked at Court. His profile spoke of a man of strength. The solid jaw line and prominent cheek bones were offset by small laughter lines around his eyes. The only hints of his angst were in the firm set of his mouth and the too-tight grip he had on the steering wheel.

She needed space or she'd fall on Court and beg for him to come with her or, worse, beg to stay. She'd once begged a man to have her and she'd promised herself she'd never do that again. Bittersweet relief filled her when Court pulled into the unloading lane of the airport. Maggie opened the door before Court had hardly pulled the car to a stop.

Getting away was what she needed to do. Find that bubble world where she knew what was going to happen day in and day out. Learn to survive without Court and make her life work again with Neetie.

Court placed their meager luggage on the curb.

Neetie hopped along beside her, saying, "Big white bird, big white bird," and pointed into the sky.

Thankful for the time to collect herself, Maggie

schooled her face so her emotions wouldn't show. All she had to do was get through the next few minutes. She looked at Court in his impeccable suit. He still commanded her attention just as he had on the day they'd met. Her heart fluttered. Now she knew those dark glasses covered the most amazing blue pools she'd ever seen. The ones that twinkled when he was kidding her, showed heartfelt concern even when he was trying to hide it, and, best of all, the ones that turned indigo as he entered her.

He felt, he cared. He just refused to admit it.

Court came to stand beside her. Her heart ached with misery. They'd gone from passionate lovers to polite acquaintances in a few short days.

"Bye, Neetie," Court said, looking down at the boy. "You do as Missy Maggie tells you."

Neetie's head bobbed up and down. Tears filled his eyes.

Maggie blinked in an effort not to join Neetie in crying. She was doing the right thing. She had to leave. Neetie needed to too. They had their own world to build now.

Court took her hand and pulled her to him. Before she realized his intent, his lips came down on hers in a searing kiss. She wrapped her arms around his neck and went up on her toes to meet him. He didn't have to ask for access to her mouth, she freely gave it and returned his hunger. Her heart burned with the pain of knowing he wouldn't be there with her the next day or the next.

As abruptly as he'd grabbed her, he let her go. "Goodbye, Maggie." He didn't look back as he slid behind the steering wheel of the car.

The cold wind of separation whirled around her, chilling her to the bone. She missed the warmth of what they'd had already. Would her tormented heart ever recover?

Court had to get away. To think. To figure out how to make the red-hot coal of agony deep within him ease. To make sure he didn't say something he would regret or, worse, didn't mean. As he pulled away from the curb, he looked into the rearview mirror. Maggie, holding Neetie's hand, stood watching him in the bright spring sunlight. His heart was back there with them. Pain burned in him. Sharp, and agonizingly bottomless. Maggie had left. She had taken Neetie with her. Court thought of them as family. His family. As far back as the day in the market when he'd stepped out to protect them, they had been his.

All of a sudden, Africa seemed like a lifetime away and life after Maggie even bleaker than Ghana in the dry season.

Court didn't know who was more surprised he'd called—his parents or him. Now he stood in front of the navy painted door of his parents' Federal-style home on Beacon Hill. Normally children didn't wait to be invited into their childhood home but this house had never really felt like home.

Maggie and Neetie had been gone for four long weeks. Daily the harsh words Maggie had thrown at him played over in his head. He'd been running. He'd known it when he'd gone to Ghana, and he knew it now. Facing Roger had been the initial step toward putting his life in order but if he was going to find any contentment he needed answers from his parents. He had to know why. Maggie dishing out some tough love had made him realize how bitter he was about his childhood. And dish it out she had. No one had ever cared about him enough to call him on what he'd been doing with his life. Even the few people he'd name as friends wouldn't have dared give a speech like the one she'd delivered.

For weeks her accusations had chafed, kept him awake at night, slipped in during his work day. Was she right? Did he need to let the past go so he could have a future?

Court was surprised when both his mother and father were there to greet him instead of their housekeeper. His father had always been a man with a commanding presence but a pleasant smile. He offered Court a hand in welcome. His mother looked the socialite she was, dressed in her designer slacks and sweater. She gave him peck on the cheek. He's seen her do the same thing many times when greeting a foundation benefactor.

"This is an unexpected surprise. Is something wrong at the foundation?"

"No, Mother. The foundation is doing fine. This is about me."

"Oh. Well, come in and tell us what's on your mind."

She led them to the formal living room. Court's smile showed no humor. He was even treated like a guest in his parents' home. It wasn't comfortable to admit but that might not be totally their fault. He'd never come around enough to be considered much more than a visitor.

"What's going on son?" his father asked as he settled into a winged-back chair.

His mother sat on the silk-covered loveseat, crossing her legs primly at the ankles while he sat in the matching chair to his father's.

Court took a deep breath. He'd be opening the old wound that had never healed. Would it be better or worse from this confrontation? "I want to talk about Lyland."

His mother gasped and looked down at her clasped hands. His father shifted in the chair.

"Why? That was so long ago," his mother said as her back went stiff as she recovered from her shock. Her boardroom persona in place, business face on.

"I know how long ago it was." Court couldn't keep the bitterness out of his voice. "He was my brother. I want to know why you shut me out. Why we never spoke of Lyland again. Why you sent me away."

Both his parents started speaking at the same time but his father held up a hand, silencing his wife. "Grace, let me talk." He looked at Court.

"We thought it was for the best. When you came home from school, we didn't want you upset. We wanted you to have happy memories."

Happy memories? The last happy memory he'd had in this house had been well before Lyland had died. His most vivid memories had all been about loneliness and the need to leave as soon as he arrived.

Grace cried softly. His father moved, taking her in his arms. "Your mother almost lost her mind after Lyland died. I finally talked her into working at the foundation to give her something to keep her sane."

"What about me?" Those words sounded juvenile and self-centered, coming from a grown man, but they were honest ones from the child he had been whose world had come apart and no one had been there to support him.

His parents look stricken, as if he slapped them. "What do you mean? We saw to your needs."

"You saw that I was fed and clothed. Sent me off to school, but I always felt like an outsider, still do. I loved Lyland too. For heaven's sake, he was my *twin* brother. I felt like I was pushed away because it was too hard to look at me and not see him. As if you wished it had been me. I was the first born, I was fine. I believed that I'd caused Lyland to be like he was."

His mother looked stricken. "Court, what made you think that?"

"Mother, I was a kid. How was I to know better? As an adult I can rationalize that it wasn't true but all those feelings…" Court tapped his chest "…are still here."

"Court, we love you as much as we loved Lyland. His problems had nothing to do with you. We wanted to protect you. We didn't want you to hurt any more than you already were."

"But I did hurt."

"We know that now." She glanced at his father. "We realized by the time you were in high school that we had gone too far. You no longer wanted to come home for holidays. By then you weren't receptive to any of our effects to connect." His mother started crying again. "As an adult you would rather be anywhere but here. We had lost both our boys."

"You could have kept trying."

"We did, in our own way. That's why we insisted you be involved in the foundation. We know you believe in the work it does, so we did everything we could think of to keep you involved. That's why we saw to it that the board voted you acting CEO when you took a leave of absence from your practice," his father said. "We thought at least we'd see you regularly. Have some interaction."

As if the shutters had been thrown open and sunlight had poured in, Court had a clearer vision of who his parents were. They loved him but their devastation over Lyland had hurt so badly that by the time they'd recovered enough to show him love, they'd lost him. Was the same thing happening between him and Maggie and Neetie? Was he repeating his parents' mistakes?

"It was never our intention to hurt you. We love you, Court," his mother said.

Court was starting to see that their strained relationship hadn't been easy on his parents but it still didn't erase all those years of hurt. He wouldn't wait twenty-five years to be clearing the air with someone he cared about. He knew his place and that was with Maggie and Neetie. It became clear what he should do. He'd go to Ghana and prove to Maggie he was worthy of her.

His mother rose and came to place her hand over his. "Court, will you give us another chance to be a part of your life? We have missed you."

He would be asking Maggie the same thing. Could he do anything less for his parents than he hoped to receive from Maggie? Court put his hand over hers. "We can try but there'll still be distance between us. I'm going to Africa to live."

A week later, Court idly tapped his pen on the large oak desk and looked out the office window at the dark clouds gathering over the harbor. The sky reminded him of the one in Ghana the day he'd driven like a madman to get Neetie back to the hospital. That simple thought brought Maggie to mind. His heart did a little tip-tap. It wouldn't be long before he saw her again. Would she have him?

Maggie let people know when she cared about them. Could he learn to be that open? With her at his side, he believed it was possible. All he had to do was convince her to take a chance on him. Maggie had given a hundred percent during their lovemaking but had always seemed to be waiting for him to offer a part of himself he hadn't been prepared to give. He'd believed he had nothing emotionally to share but now he knew differently. He was through protecting his heart. It belonged to Maggie anyway. He'd have to trust her to care for it.

This was his last day as CEO of the Armstrong Foundation. He had resigned. It was time to start fighting for what he wanted in his life. He wanted Maggie and Neetie. He wanted them to be his family. He wanted Neetie to have a sense of belonging, to know he had acceptance and love. All the things Court hadn't had as a child. He wouldn't repeat the mistakes of his parents. He would support and care for them during the tough times, not push them away.

Once again the desire to practice medicine had become a burning need. He was eager to return to the hospital in Ghana. The work there had been rewarding. By working with the Mamprusi he would honor Lyland's memory, help those that needed it most and use his influence to improve the hospital. It was time to stop wasting his skills and talent.

He and his parents still didn't have the parent-and-son relationship that they should but they were working at it. It would take a long time to ease all the years of hurt and estrangement. He had learned from his parents' mistakes. Instead of wishing for life to be different, he planned to actively work at making his different. He planned to concentrate on what he could build with Maggie and Neetie, instead of dwelling on what had been.

Court's family lived in Ghana and he was going there to be with them. The cadence of the pen picked up. Would they welcome him home?

CHAPTER TEN

MAGGIE glanced at the plane circling to land. It would contain the next installment of doctors to the revolving door of medical staff that the hospital still experienced. She was grateful for the help but nothing had changed regarding assistance for the hospital.

She'd given up any hope of receiving any financial support from the Armstrong Foundation. She and Neetie had been home two months and the hospital had heard nothing about the resubmitted application. The hospital would have to carry on as it had for years and hope that eventually some supporter would understand the value of the work being done in Teligu.

They'd heard nothing from Court. Maggie didn't expect she would but she still wished for some contact—every day. She shook her head, trying to clear it, which was almost impossible. The only time Court wasn't in the forefront of her thoughts was when she was working. Because of those memories she'd volunteered for any extra shifts or chores that needed to be done. If she was exhausted, then she slept.

She could stand here wishing for something that was never to be or see to the patients waiting. "Next," she said in Mamprusi, and waved the next person toward the doctor's examination table. She glanced to where Neetie played with some friends under a shed used as the nutritional clinic that morning. She had received the final papers making Neetie hers the day before. She smiled. Neetie filled her life with joy but a void still remained that only Court could fill. She missed Court with an ache that didn't ease. "Please sit on the table," she told the woman, turning to get the BP cuff.

"I'll do her heart and respiration while you see to her BP."

Court.

Maggie went stock-still, her breath caught in her throat. It couldn't be but she'd know that deep, rusty timbre anywhere. It replayed in her head very night before she dropped off to sleep. The woman's name she was trying to write on the paper became a mess of wiggly lines. The pencil fell from her hand to the floor but she still didn't look at him. She was afraid she'd make a fool of herself by jumping into his arms.

His arm hair tickled her skin when he brushed against her as he placed the pencil on the counter. Maggie shivered as her body heated up.

"You'll have to look at me some time," Court whispered, close enough to her ear that it was almost a kiss. She wished it had been. "Maggie, we have a patient waiting."

Court knew her well enough to know that would bring her round. He stepped to the patient and began listening to her heart. Maggie went to the other side of the table and put the BP cuff on the woman's thin arm.

"Why're you here, Court?" she asked in a shaky voice as she pumped the bulb on the blood-pressure cuff.

"Raja needed a ride home."

Her heart, already filled with joy, expanded with more. Her head jerked up, meeting his gaze. He made that statement like he was a taxi driver who made flights into Teligu once a week.

He smiled and there was tenderness, caring and something she didn't dare put a name to in his beautiful blue eyes. "You can see her when we finish here."

She glanced at the people waiting in line. Could she wait that long?

His smile grew. "Go on, I'll handle things here until you get back. She's waiting just outside. Don't be gone long."

"You can't just fly in and start telling me what to do."

He chuckled. "I've missed you, Missy Maggie." His words were low, almost a caress. He came around the table and nudged her toward the door. "Go and see Raja. I'll be here for you to lambast when you get back."

It was difficult for Court to concentrate on his patient when he could hear the high chatter of the women seeing each other for the first time in months.

Raja had quickly adapted to the state-of-the-art artificial leg. The weeks of physical therapy had paid off. She was walking well and starting to run. It was gratifying to have been a part of seeing that she had a chance at some semblance of a normal life.

Maggie reentered the examining room, as he'd finished up with the patient and she was leaving. The bright smile on Maggie's face made his heart swell. With no inhibitions, Maggie walked up to him, wrapped her arms around his neck and hugged him. "Thank you. Thank you."

"I think you can do better than that." He dipped his head and caught her lips with his.

Maggie leaned into him, and he angled his head so that he could capture her mouth fully. The sound of someone climbing onto the examination table forced him to pull away. Maggie's soft sigh made him want to go back for more. Maybe he still had a chance.

He said to his patient, "She attacked me."

The man offered a broad smile, showing the few teeth he owned. "My wives do the same thing to me."

Court chuckled, and Maggie went an attractive shade of crimson.

She stepped away and became all business but Court noticed the tremor of her hands as she cared for the old man. A couple of times he caught her looking at him overtly. A rattled Maggie was an irresistibly lovely Maggie. He had missed her so and was ready to be done with clinic so he could get her in his arms again.

"Have you seen Neetie?" she asked as another patient made his way toward them.

"Not yet. I thought he must be in school and I didn't want to disturb him. I'll go find him as soon as we're finished here."

"He'll be so excited you're here. He's missed you."

"Have you missed me, Maggie?"

Pink touched her cheeks, and she looked at him longingly before she turned her back, acting as if something of great importance was on the counter. "Yes, I've missed you." The answer was little more than a whisper but he'd heard what his heart desperately needed to know.

The tension built between them as they worked in the small space. A brush of a hand when he requested a supply, the closeness of their bodies as she passed on the way to the cabinet, to the look in Maggie's eyes when their gazes met had Court wanting to grab her and find the nearest private corner. Thankfully the line of patients dwindled and they only had a few more to see or he might embarrass them both. Not soon enough, the last patient left.

Court caught Maggie's hand and pulled her toward the door, closing it. Leaning back against it, he drew her to him. It felt marvelous to have her touching him. This was where he belonged. In Maggie's arms. In Ghana. He'd come home. Court took a deep breath, inhaling the sweet smell of wildflowers in her hair. With a tug of the band, the mass of brown bounty fell around her shoulders. His hands ran through it and held her face so that he could look into her eyes. They had gone wide with surprise.

Maggie blinked. The surprise was replaced by expectancy, desire and welcome. She shifted toward him, and that was enough of a silent offer.

He brought her lips to his, maneuvering until the perfect connection was found. The link he'd been missing. The one he'd been so desperate to find again over the past long weeks. Maggie gave herself and he gratefully accepted, his tongue mating with hers. A gentle sound of pleasure came from her as she pressed closer. Small fingers crept over his chest in a kneading motion until they clenched about his neck.

Knocking on the door vaguely caught Court's attention but his focus remained on the wet, welcoming lips beneath his.

The knock became a banging against the thin wood. "Mommy Maggie, Mommy Maggie."

Court knew that voice. He'd missed the kid too.

Mommy Maggie suited her. She mothered everyone. Always tried to make everything right. She was what made his world right.

Maggie stepped away, put a finger to Court's lips and smiled. She called to Neetie, "Just a minute, honey. I've got a surprise for you."

Court smiled down at her and let her pull him away from the door. She searched for her hair band and found it on the floor. Flipping her head over, she retied her hair. "It's not because I have to put my hair in order."

He looked at her as if he didn't believe her.

"I've gotten better about letting it be messy. I don't want people asking questions about what we've been doing because my hair is down," she whispered.

"I wouldn't care."

"I'm sure you wouldn't." She pulled open the door. "Look who's here."

When Court stepped out from behind the door Neetie yelped, "Mister Doctor," and jumped into Court's open arms.

"Hey, buddy. It's good to see you." Court hugged Neetie as tightly as the boy was hugging him.

It had almost killed her to leave Court, and it would assuredly be the same when he'd gone this time, but she couldn't help but be glad to see him. She'd known loneliness that was bone-achingly deep and constant since she'd left him in Boston. With him in Teligu, it was like a part of her had been found. She would embrace him, love him, for however long he was there.

"Mommy Maggie?" Court asked her over Neetie's shoulder.

She smiled. "It is official."

"That's great."

The boy let Court go, and he stood.

"I live with Mommy Maggie now. She take care of me always." Neetie took her hand and looked at Court.

"I know she will," Court said, to her more than to Neetie. "She is good at taking care of people."

"We move. I have my own room like your house."

"You do?" Court gave Maggie a questioning look.

"When Neetie came to live with me, I asked for one of the family bungalows. They're usually reserved for visiting doctors. Those staying long term."

"I'm glad you got one when you did because none will be available now."

"Why's that?"

"Because I brought a couple of long-term doctors with me."

"Really, Court? That's wonderful." She grabbed his hand. "How?"

"The Armstrong Foundation is going to pay doctors and nurses for as long as needed, while at the same time offering scholarships to the Mamprusi people to go to medical and nursing school. The understanding is that they'll work four years here to repay schooling. The hope is they'll want to stay by that time."

"Oh, that sounds wonderful. It's an even better plan than I had in mind."

"I thought you might like it."

"I need to go—"

"No, you don't." He enclosed her arm with a gentle hand. "This time let someone else do it.

We need to talk. About us. Neetie, Raja is wait-ing at the mess hall for you. She needs someone to eat dinner with, and I brought you something special."

"What is it? What is it?" Neetie asked, skipping around Court legs.

The boy almost vibrated with excitement. He'd been getting stronger everyday they had been back. Maggie knew how Neetie felt. Court cre-ated the same thrill in her.

"How would you like a little ice cream after supper?"

Neetie shouted, "Ya," and was running down the path toward the mess hall before she and Court stepped out of the building.

Court grinned as he watched the boy then he turned to her. "Where can we talk that we won't be interrupted?"

"I guess we could go to my bungalow."

"Hey, Maggie," one of the nurses called, "can you help me put up bandages before you go to dinner?"

Court's harsh word came out sharp and blunt at the same time.

Before Maggie could answer, Court took her

hand in his and pulled her in the direction of the shed where the trucks were parked. He left her no choice but to go along. She didn't know what he had in mind, and it didn't matter. She was just glad to have him there.

Court spoke to the man who handled maintenance on the vehicles. The man nodded then pointed to the big truck they had driven to the village. Court headed for the vehicle.

"What're you doing?"

"Making sure we're not disturbed," he said with impatience.

"But Neetie?"

"Neetie will be fine. Raja is looking after him."

He opened the passenger door, unceremoniously picked her up and sat her in the seat. She received a quick kiss before he slammed the door closed and jogged around the truck.

"Where're we going?" she asked as he cranked the truck.

"I don't know. Just away from here."

They had been riding west for thirty minutes and Maggie knew little more than she had when they'd left the hospital compound. She wasn't complaining. Having Court hold her hand seemed like heaven and they could drive forever as long as he was with her. The truck jerked to a sudden stop. She might have bumped her head on the windshield if Court hadn't let go of her hand and put his arm out to hold her in place.

She twisted round in the seat to face him. "Being a little dramatic today, Doctor?"

"I have to get you alone. I could've proposed at a Red Sox game and had fewer interruptions," he muttered.

She might have laughed at him if it hadn't been for the heart-stopping word—*propose*.

"What do you mean, propose?" Maggie hardly dared to breathe.

Court acted as if he hadn't heard her. She watched his chest expand as he took a gulp of air. He scrubbed his hand across his face. "Could I be doing a lousier job of this?"

"What's going on, Court?"

Taking both of her hands in his, he looked at her. "I'm trying, in the most inept way I can imagine, to tell you that I want you to marry me."

Her heart galloped.

"I can't live without you." He sounded amazed by the concept.

"I love you too but you know I'm needed here. You have obligations in Boston. We'd end up making each other miserable. Never seeing each other. And it's not only me any more. I have Neetie to consider."

He squeezed her hands. "I want Neetie too. And living here won't be a problem. I'm staying here."

"What about your work at the foundation?" She hesitated. "What about your practice?"

"Dad's taking the CEO position again so the foundation doesn't need me. I'll be overseeing the work done here on its behalf. And I sold my practice."

"What? You can't quit medicine. You're too fine a doctor. You need to be helping people, it's who you are."

Court put a finger across her lips. "Hush, and let me explain." Taking her hand again, he said, "I had a good long think after you left. I started facing my demons where Jimmy was concerned. Even talked to my parents. Things are better between us—still not great but we're working on it." The dry tone in his voice was a contrast to the emotion in his eyes.

She gripped his hands. "I'm proud of you."

"I became a doctor to honor my brother and now Jimmy. To help others. It's time I start doing that again. I've never felt better about myself than when I was here, working with you. There are plenty of doctors in Boston to care for people but here I'm needed."

Did she dare to hope? "What're you trying to say?"

"I'm telling you that I'm not giving up medicine, I'm just giving up my Boston practice. I'm going to practice here at the hospital. A permanent doctor for as long as I'm needed. Here I can make a real difference. This is where I found peace, doing what I love, and most important of all here is where you are. And Neetie. Make it perfect and say you'll marry me."

Those eyes she loved so much looked at her earnestly, beseechingly, as if he feared she might say no.

"So did you say how you feel about me?"

"Honey, I love you." Those were words she'd never thought she'd hear him say.

"Will you say them again?"

He smiled. "Was I that bad about sharing my feelings?"

She nodded.

"I love you. I love you. I love you."

"Sounds just right. If I marry you, can I have your leather chair?"

He pretended to think hard about it. "How about we continue to share it? I'll have it shipped here."

"Deal," she said, sealing the agreement with a kiss.

Minutes and one incredibly delightful kiss later he asked, "So that I'm clear, you have agreed to marry me?"

"Yes. Just try to get away." She pulled him to her again.

Court tucked Maggie closer as they lay on the truck bed, watching the sun slip below the horizon. The soft drumming of rain on the tarp made the moment more intimate.

"Are you sure that you want to give up Boston for this?" Maggie asked with a sigh.

"I thought I made that clear a few minutes ago."

She kissed his neck, then put her chin on his chest and looked up at him. "You might have to do a little more convincing."

He cupped her bare behind and pulled her toward him. "I think I can handle that," he said, before kissing her deeply and passionately, more than willing to do some convincing. Not breaking contact, Court maneuvered her on top of him, before she broke the kiss.

"I need to ask you something."

"Now?" He moved his hips in question.

"I don't think it should wait."

He stopped fondling her breast and looked at her. The serious tone of her voice had him question whether or not he wanted to hear what she had to say.

"Um, how do you feel about adding a few more children to our family?"

"Do you have any in mind?"

"I might."

"Honey, whatever you want, I want. A houseful, if that will make you happy."

She wrapped her arms around his neck, and shimmied farther up him. "I love you."

"I think maybe you should show it." His hand drifted across her hip.

"I believe I should." Maggie leaned down and said against his mouth, "You'll be a wonderful father," before she showed him with her lips what he meant to her.

Court had found the contentment and acceptance in this stark land he'd so longed for. It had hidden the jewel that made his life complete. Maggie's dream had been to have a family and together they would make that dream come true, surrounded by a lifetime of love.

* * * * *